"**Beehives** begins with a bang, and nothing is what it appears to be when a mysterious hermit's death detours Jamie Aldrich's romantic holiday with fiancé Sam Mazie into a dangerous discovery of long-ago secrets and modern-day treachery. Don't miss this latest in Mary Coley's Family Secret Series."

—Loulou Harrington
Author of *Murder, Mayhem and Bliss*
and *Murder Most Thorny*

"With her potent spell of Oklahoma's natural beauty and human nature's sticky depths, Mary Coley lures her readers into a tale as intricate and agitated as the Beehives of her title."

—Sara Kay Rupnik
Author of *Women Longing to Fly*

"In **Beehives**, Mary Coley has put together an engaging story rich with Oklahoma history, immersing the reader in the natural beauty of Green Country and keeping the mystery going until the end."

—Joshua Danker-Dake
Author of *The Retail*

In Jamie Aldrich, Nancy Drew meets Anna Pigeon and becomes more cerebral and stronger than them both. In **Beehives**, Jamie's sedate getaway in a state park in the Crosstimbers turns into a red hot burn. Read the book but watch out for the bees!

—Jackson Burnett
Author of *The Past Never Ends*

What Others Are Saying About Mary Coley's
Cobwebs
(from Amazon reviews)

Cobwebs made me delightfully uneasy and kept me in suspense. I highly recommend it to suspense lovers.

—Jackie D.

On the edge of your seat suspense! This book is a great quick read. Jamie's twists, turns and mishaps in finding out the story of her great aunt Elizabeth keep you anxious to turn the page.

—Terri

Cobwebs takes an intriguing journey into dark places, family secrets, and into the forgotten history of the Osage oil boom. Mary Coley has written a fine novel of suspense and mystery that will keep you up into the late hours of the night.

—Jackson Burnett

The mystery was well plotted, the characters well drawn and compelling.

—Sherrill Nilson

Here is a new thriller by a fresh talent that will genuinely keep you on the edge of your seat

—Glen V. McIntyre

Cobwebs is a beautiful suspense novel on so many levels. Once I started reading the story I was captured in the lovely silken web of words that this writer weaves so well.

—J. Rhine

Beehives

Beehives

a suspense novel

MARY COLEY

Beehives: A Suspense Novel

Published by Wheatmark®
1760 East River Road, Suite 145, Tucson, Arizona 85718 USA
www.wheatmark.com

ISBN: 978-1-62787-313-0 (paperback)
ISBN: 978-1-62787-314-7 (ebook)
LCCN: 2015946250

I dedicate this book to the young men of the Civilian Conservation Corps in Oklahoma. 5000 men served in this state, in 26 different camps.

These young craftsmen created amazing parks for the people of Oklahoma. I have lived in several Oklahoma communities where CCC-built facilities are located. The familiar rock picnic shelters, walls and curving stairways they created in lush, green parks have endured the tests of time. Countless children have played on the wide lawns surrounding these structures and thousands of families have gathered together to celebrate 'family' in the eighty-plus years since they were constructed.

I also dedicate this book to my husband, Daryl. His unflinching acceptance of the demands of my writing/ editing/ marketing schedule is deserving of an award.

Acknowledgments

Thank you to Nick Conner, ranger and park manager at Osage Hills State Park for speaking with me about this beautiful park, its facilities and history.

Park Information: 2131 Osage Hills Park Road, Pawhuska, OK 74056. 918-336-4141. OsageHills@travelok.com

Thank you to Donna Horton, retired senior naturalist at the Oxley Nature Center in Tulsa, Oklahoma, for sharing her beekeeping expertise with me. Oxley is located in Tulsa's largest park, Mohawk Park.

Mailing address is: Box 150209, Tulsa, OK 74115; email:oxley@cityoftulsa.org; phone: 918-669-6644; website: http://www.oxleynaturecenter.org.

Thank you to Sergeant Middleton of the Tulsa Police Departments K-9 division, and to Deanna Butler of the Eastern Oklahoma K-9 Search Team for their help with my questions about the Search and Rescue (SAR) process and the training and behavior of canine officers.

Thank you to the Oklahoma Historical Society for providing easy access to information about the CCC and the WPA projects in Oklahoma.

And finally, thanks to my critique team and beta readers who offered so many great tips for ways to make this story better: Sara Kay Rupnik, Ada Harrington, Joshua Danker-Dake, Mark Darrah, Jackie King, Paula Alfred and Jennifer Adolf. This book wouldn't have been possible without you.

"Teddy Bear, Teddy Bear" – A Jump Rope Rhyme

Teddy Bear, Teddy Bear, Turn around.
Teddy Bear, Teddy Bear, Touch the ground.
Teddy Bear, Teddy Bear, Touch your shoe.
Teddy Bear, Teddy Bear, That will do.
Teddy Bear, Teddy Bear, Go upstairs.
Teddy Bear, Teddy Bear, Say your prayers.
Teddy Bear, Teddy Bear, Turn out the light.
Teddy Bear, Teddy Bear, Say goodnight.

CAST OF CHARACTERS

Jamie Aldrich – a widowed science teacher, engaged to Sam

Sam Mazie – an attorney and member of the Osage Tribe

Doug Moyer – a park ranger

Roy Snyder – the park manager

Sheriff John Standingbear – the Osage County sheriff

Celeste – the park's seasonal naturalist

Chip Erikson – one of the park's maintenance staff

Stephen Knapp – Sam's cousin, and a beekeeper

Aiden Blunt – a historian, in the park to research the CCC camp

Betty and Barnard Wood – a Wichita couple, staying in a park cabin

Jason and Crystal Hargis – a Tulsa couple, staying in a park cabin

Jacob and Emma Hargis – the Hargis children. Emma, 11; Jacob 9.

Suzanne and Michael Bales – an Oklahoma City couple camping in the park

Bridget Halsted – a former teacher living as a hermit at Osage Hills State Park

PROLOGUE

The gray-haired woman huddled in the blackness of the sumac thicket as rain hammered down on the forest.

With slick, trembling fingers she reached toward the wound on her head.

Ow.

She stared at her hand, trying to focus on the red smear on her fingertips. Slowly, she rubbed her fingers on her jeans, on the filthy denim covered with grass, bits of leaves and twigs. She peered up at the thick canopy of the trees and the curtain of rain, but saw only a veil of vibrating green. She closed her eyes; her body swayed.

Hurts. So bad.

Lightning flashed above her. It flashed again, and again. She squeezed her eyes shut even tighter.

Make it stop. God, make it stop.

Thunder shook the ground. She grasped the wispy branches of the sumac, lost her balance, and fell.

Teddy bear, teddy bear . . . The rhyme played in her head as the rain pounded. She rolled to her hands and knees. She crawled from the thicket to the base of the nearest tree.

Help. Need help. Anyone. Ooh.

Pain buzzed in her ears, filling her head.

Bees? My bees?

Behind the white noise of the rain, a voice called. "Bridget? Where are you?"

Patrick? No. He's gone. Gone.

"Bridget? Come out."

Close, so close.

Her body shook.

Hide. Where?

She inched her way up from the base of the trunk until she was standing straight, pressed against the thick rough bark of the giant oak. She lifted her head and let the rain pelt her face.

Oh, such pain. My head.

Her world spun, a mass of tumbling green and shimmering silver rain. She turned her face into the tree, feeling the wood bite into her soft cheek.

Help, Patrick. Now.

Climb.

CHAPTER 1

Friday, May 17, 2001

Sam and I pushed through the thick undergrowth crowding the shadowy nature trail. Around us, moisture dripped from the leaves of the tall oaks and hickory trees of northern Oklahoma's Osage Hills State Park. I shivered in my flannel sweatshirt, wishing I had worn a rain slicker or a hoodie.

"Maybe we should go back to the cabin until later in the day," I suggested. "It's still so wet." The humid air clung to my face and my nose itched. May in these thick humid forests was synonymous with ticks, chiggers, and mosquitoes. I was willing to ignore the insects, though. I was here to spend much-needed time with Sam to plan our future together, and that meant a few nights in a rustic cabin in a state park. I scratched my nose.

Even though the storm had ended hours ago, raindrops still dripped from the trees, splashing into puddles on the narrow gravel path.

Sam focused his shining brown-black eyes on me. "Really? My 'nature lover' wants to spend this beautiful spring morning inside?" He smiled, showing straight white teeth in a full-lipped mouth that was framed by brown skin.

My heart kicked. The still-new diamond engagement ring on my left ring finger flashed as it caught a stray beam of sunlight passing through an opening in the thick canopy. I was a divorcée, a widow, and now soon to be a bride for the third time.

Sam touched my cheek. "I can only think of one thing I want to do inside a cabin with you this time of day." He leaned in for a kiss, smoothing my hair and lifting it over my shoulders.

A grin spread across my face as well as a blush as I kissed the man who had made life worth living again. My despair after my husband Ben's death had been impenetrable, a thick, heavy drape I had been unable to push aside. Since Sam had come into my life last spring, life had been new again, like fresh air after weeks in a dank cave. Our relationship had grown, nourished by daily phone calls and monthly visits as we continued to live six hundred miles apart.

In this moment, I had no regrets about finishing my contract to teach high school science for Las Vegas, New Mexico Public Schools, even though it had meant a physical separation. During those months, I'd found closure for my life with Ben. My future belonged to Sam, my handsome Osage attorney.

Water dripped onto my forehead. I swiped at it. The clear moisture evaporated on my fingertips in a sudden gust of wind that rustled the leaves.

The air vibrated. Birds fluttered up into the sky. The trees creaked.

CCRRAACCKK!

Sam shoved me to the mossy ground and partially covered me with his body.

A huge limb crashed down; the ground beneath us shook. Long-dead twigs and loose bark shot up into the air, only to rain down seconds later.

All sounds of life in the forest—chirping frogs and crickets as well as tweeting birds—ceased.

I gasped for breath; Sam rolled into a crouch. He peered up at the sixty-foot trees above. "Damn it, that was too close."

I thought about the Oklahoma weather reports I'd watched from New Mexico the previous month in anticipation of my trip here. The forecasters had talked about what an exceptionally rainy spring it had been because the jet stream was tracking so far south. That dead branch had become waterlogged by all this rain.

A brown creeper broke the silence. The little bird chirped as it flitted to the wide, jagged scar on the nearest tree trunk. It pecked at the newly opened split in the tree's peeling bark.

Sam helped me to my feet, brushing leaf litter from my sleeves. I did the same for his shoulders and arms, taking special care to rub a smear of dirt from his face and another from the turquoise ring on his right hand.

On the ground nearby, the thick, twisted tree limb extended twenty feet, with side branches reaching into the underbrush like arthritic fingers.

"Hello? Everyone okay?" Rapid footsteps crunched on the forest path and a tall, slender man in a green khaki uniform and stiff-brimmed hat emerged from the trees. The park ranger surveyed the fallen branch. "Whoa! That's what just fell? You folks all right?"

"We're fine," Sam said. "But we might not have been. We were standing right under it."

"That rain last night was the third heavy storm we've had in the past two weeks," the ranger said, shaking his head. "Dead limbs drop from these old trees after nearly every one of them."

Right on cue, another gust of wind rattled the tree branches and another loud crack vibrated the air. In the distance, someone screamed.

The park ranger took off running toward the sound; Sam and I scrambled after him.

A quarter of a mile down the trail, another enormous broken limb lay among smashed plants on the forest floor. One end of the thirty-foot branch was caught in the yoke of a tree; the remainder stretched across the nature trail and into the forest on the opposite side.

The ranger stopped several yards short of the fallen limb and lifted his hand. "Wait." He walked down the sloping path. The broken limb, more than a foot in diameter, had snapped in two and dug into the soft earth close to the trail. He studied the ground.

Sam and I inched closer.

An elderly woman lay just off the trail, her ribcage smashed beneath the limb. Her eyes stared vacantly toward the sky.

CHAPTER 2

The ranger squatted beside the body and then leaned over to place two fingers on the woman's left carotid artery.

"She's dead." He pulled a radio transmitter from his belt while glancing at a GPS device he had pulled from his shirt pocket with his other hand. Speaking into the radio, he gave our location and then said, "Send the medical examiner with the sheriff." He reattached the radio to his belt. Arms crossed, he frowned at the woman.

She wore a faded green and blue plaid flannel shirt. Her legs, which jutted out from the other side of the tree branch, were covered by well-worn jeans; a patch covered one knee. Mud, twigs, and plant debris coated blue slip-on walking shoes. Her wet, tangled gray hair splayed out onto the mossy rock beneath her, and a crust of black, dried blood matted her hair and upper forehead. A huge purple and red bruise covered her left cheek.

I closed my eyes to block out the image of her face, but it was painted onto the backs of my eyelids.

"If she was alive," the ranger muttered, "I'd be introducing you to Bridget, our resident hermit."

I blinked, frozen in place by the shock of the woman's death here, next to the path. Beside me, Sam cleared his throat.

"A recluse?" he asked. "She lived here in the park?"

The ranger tromped around her through the foliage and

over to the tree, then back to the path. "Been here thirty years or more, so I've heard."

Static broke in over the ranger's radio transmitter and he pulled the device from his belt again. "I'll wait," he said into it.

A cardinal trilled a few notes from the top of a green ash tree. I rubbed my arms, feeling cold in the damp air despite my sweatshirt. Green leaves and tree trunks pressed in from every direction; I sucked air in, feeling suffocated.

"You know," the man began, "I've been the ranger here for nearly five years, and this is the first time anything like this has happened." A muscle in his cheek twitched as he glanced at the body again.

I allowed myself to look at the woman one more time before I averted my eyes. My heart pounded as if I had been running for miles. "It's shocking," I said. I meant it with every ounce of my being, and I'd seen my share of dead bodies this past year. Swaying, I leaned against Sam.

His arm closed around me as he accepted my weight. He stroked my hair and kissed the top of my head. "I'm sorry, sweetheart."

He was on the same wavelength I was, thinking about all that had happened since we reunited a year ago. First, my great aunt's brush with death and the complex web of hate and deceit we had uncovered in her and Sam's hometown, and then, late last summer, my experience with the human trafficking ring that had kidnapped my stepdaughter.

Questions about the old woman pounded in my head. I squeezed my eyes shut and reminded myself that I didn't need to get involved in this. We were only here for a few days. After that, this incident, this strange death in the forest, would be forgotten. I worked at regaining my focus: the wedding I was planning with Sam. The humid air pressed in, the birds twittered, a gnat fluttered against my cheek.

"I didn't introduce myself," the ranger said, pulling me out of my thoughts. "I'm Doug Moyer." He took off his hat.

I looked at the young man. His tanned face was smooth,

his eyebrows bushy, and his wide-set eyes untroubled by what had just happened. I could hardly catch my breath. My stomach roiled when I glanced at the dead woman again amidst the heavy odor of mold and decay.

"I'm Sam Mazie, and this is my fiancée, Jamie Aldrich."

Doug Moyer turned his back to the body. "I hope you won't let this ruin your visit. It's supposed to be great weather all week."

"My cousin Stephen Knapp suggested the park as a getaway. It's been awhile since I've been here. And it's Jamie's first trip to Osage Hills." Sam smiled at me, and my mouth twitched into a small grin. A dead woman lay only a few feet away. Was the ranger going to make small talk? Maybe it was the only way he knew to cope with an unexpected death in the park.

"Knapp? We've met," Moyer said. His voice cracked and he cleared his throat. "I couldn't do what he does, though. Bees and I don't get along." He flicked absently at the side of his neck as if he were shooing away an insect.

Bees. Sam had told me all about his cousin, an organic farmer and beekeeper. Mouth dry, I wished for a drink of water, dry air, and a wide, blue New Mexico sky.

"He's got a group of hives in a meadow not far from the park's lake," Moyer said. His radio crackled and he turned away to talk privately, striding up the trail as he listened.

"I'm sorry about this, honey," Sam said. "This is not what I'd imagined our morning hike would be like." He laced his fingers with mine.

The ranger returned to us. "I'll have to get a formal state-ment from you both later today." Filtered sunlight glinted on the ranger's short, thick walnut-colored hair. Bits of gold specked his brown eyes. The muscles in his neck bunched and then relaxed.

"We'll be around." Sam glanced at his watch and turned to me. "Stephen will be at the cabin soon. Remember, I'm going with him to see his hives. Are you coming?"

I shook my head. I was interested in the beekeeping process, but I would stay as far away from the bees as I could while Stephen was messing with their hives. I thought of the hermit. "Tell us more about Bridget."

"Supposedly, her lover died here. She couldn't get over it. Eventually, she moved out here to live." Doug Moyer's swallow sounded like a gulp; he rubbed the back of his neck. Beads of sweat glistened on his forehead.

"Near here?" Sam peered into the trees around us.

The ranger cleared his throat again. "Near enough." He picked at something on his trousers and then shifted from one foot to the other.

In the distance, an engine revved. Seconds later, an ATV pulling a small trailer emerged through the underbrush on the path, followed by a second ATV. The vehicles stopped, and two men hopped from each.

One pair scurried to the body, carrying duffle bags of equipment; each man wore a black windbreaker jacket with *Medical Examiner* written in white on the back. The other two men were dressed in green khaki uniforms like Moyer. As they walked toward us, the older man, several inches shorter and several pounds heavier than the ranger, scowled at us from beneath the brim of an olive-green baseball cap.

"Roy Snyder, Park Superintendent," he said. "And you are . . .?"

Sam introduced us as he shook the man's hand.

"I was with these folks down the trail a ways when this branch fell," Doug Moyer said, gesturing toward the fallen limb. "We all headed here. They were with me when I found Bridget."

"You were hiking? After that downpour early this morning?" Snyder frowned at Sam and me. The already-deep lines in his forehead and around his eyes told me he did a lot of frowning.

"We were out enjoying the park. That's what we came for." Sam gave me a look that warmed my heart. "We'll move on and let you all take care of business. We are in cabin seven if you need to talk to us."

"I'm sure we'll want to talk to you." Snyder directed his gravelly voice at Sam. "The sheriff should be along soon. Stay in the park." His attention shifted to the smashed body in the undergrowth just off the trail. "Jesus, Mary, and Joseph." He pulled the ball cap off his head and held it by the brim as he studied the body.

An engine roared not far away, and seconds later, a black four-wheel-drive SUV with *Osage County Sheriff* painted on the side doors burst through the bushes beside the trail and jerked to a stop. A thirty-something Native American man hopped out and walked around the vehicle to where we waited. Two other deputies exited the vehicle.

"John Standingbear, Osage County Sheriff," the man said to me, rapidly shaking my hand and then Sam's. "Good to see you again, Sam. You and Ranger Moyer found the body?"

"Yes," Sam replied. "My fiancée and I were hiking."

The sheriff nodded at me. His glance did not linger on the nearby body. "Did anyone see Bridget in the forest before this happened?"

Moyer cleared his throat. "Haven't had a chance to investigate anything yet, Sheriff. I'm happy to interview any and all park visitors if you'd like to know if anyone saw her earlier today."

"Any idea about cause of death?" Sheriff Standingbear asked.

"The branch fell on her," Moyer said. "Looks pretty cut and dried to me."

The sheriff peered around the site before he glared at Doug Moyer. "And it looks like someone tramped around here recently."

Snyder glowered at the ranger. "Was it you?"

Doug Moyer opened his mouth, but Sheriff Standingbear spoke. "We'll handle the investigation, Roy," he said. "For now, let's let the medical examiner do his job. We'll keep you informed." He motioned toward his deputies, who were placing small yellow flags around the area and taking photographs.

"Anyone else here when you arrived? Did you notice anything unusual?" Standingbear asked Sam and me.

I shook my head, and Sam and Doug Moyer shook theirs.

"Lots of park visitors make this trail loop," Moyer said. "Dozens every day."

The sheriff moved up the path to Bridget's body.

"You've got your work cut out for you, John," Snyder called to the sheriff. "Moyer can help if you need him."

"Thanks," the sheriff shot back over his shoulder. "He can talk to all the cabin residents. We'll interview those using the tent and RV campgrounds. Someone saw something." Standingbear turned his attention to his men, who were rigging ropes in preparation to hoist the limb from where it had fallen.

"If you don't need us, we'll head back to the cabin," Sam said. "I'm sure Jamie could use a break." He smoothed my hair, tucking it behind my ear.

I was more than ready to get back to the cabin. We'd only arrived last night; this was not a good way to begin a five-day vacation to plan our future.

"Thanks, Mr. Mazie," Moyer said. "Give me another good hour here, and then I'll let you know what we need from you in the way of a statement."

Sam led me down the path and away from the men, his hand warm and snug in mine.

Behind us, Snyder barked orders to Doug Moyer. I imagined the work in store for him and the deputies, the gruesome task of lifting the thick branch to retrieve the body.

"He can't be a pleasant man to work for," I muttered. Why was that always my first reaction to men in command?

We wound our way in and out of the trees on our way back to the cabin area, passing meadows where bright yellow-green spring grasses grew. I pushed my mind away from Bridget and thought about all I knew of the rugged area known as the Cross Timbers. The region covered parts of Eastern Oklahoma, Arkansas, and Missouri with scrubby oak trees, mostly black-jack and post oak. Early explorers and pioneers had named the region for these nearly impenetrable forests.

Occasionally, the woods opened into small meadows like the ones we were passing, where prairie grasses reached their long roots deep into the thick soil. In areas with abundant moisture, other trees—hickory, ash, walnut, mulberry, and elm—grew with various species of oaks to create beautiful forests.

After Sam and I were married, I would get my Oklahoma teaching certificate and teach science again. So many young people in my classes—as well as their parents—had been afraid to be outside. No one had ever taught them about ecology, ecosystems and how they work, or about the fascinating creatures we share the earth with.

Sam jerked to a stop in time for us to catch a glimpse of a family of deer peering through the trees at us. Seconds later, the trio bounded away, disappearing on the other side of a small clearing. A squirrel chattered from the boll of a tree twenty feet away.

A shiver ran down my back. My mind replayed our brief race down the path to the scene of Bridget's death, and the image of her mottled purple cheek flashed into my head. Had she looked up and known what was about to happen?

"Someone screamed when that limb fell." I locked eyes with Sam. "What if it wasn't Bridget? What if someone else was there? Do you think the ranger thought of that?"

"I guess we'll have to wait and see if the scream is brought up in the investigation." He ran his fingers up and down my back and then grabbed my hand as he started down the path again. "I don't want to talk about it anymore. I won't let it ruin our time together here."

Sam may not have wanted to talk about it, but that didn't keep me from thinking about it. A hermit living in a state park. Why? My brain conjured up all kinds of scenario.

CHAPTER 3

Ten minutes later, we stepped off the tree-shaded trail and into an open area. Mowed lawns stretched in every direction, interspersed with stone and log cabins, each with its own patio, cooking grill, short driveway, and lawn. The mixed scents of cut grass and burning charcoal floated in the air. From the park's brochure, I had learned that seventy years ago, men enrolled in the Civilian Conservation Corps had constructed the facilities in the park.

Thoughts of the dead woman flooded my mind again. I wanted to erase my memory picture of her broken body, smashed beneath the tree limb, but the image clung there.

As we crossed the lawn toward cabin seven, a man rose from the picnic table near our cabin's outdoor fireplace and waved.

"Hey, Sam," he called. "How are you, buddy?" Smiling, our guest leaned against the picnic table and waited for us.

Stephen was as Sam had described him, of average height and skinny, his toasted skin and black hair revealing his Native American ancestry.

The two men shook hands.

"Jamie, I'm glad to meet you," Stephen said. He hugged me quickly. Stephen gestured beyond the circle of cabins toward the main road. "What's going on?" he asked. "I saw an ambulance and a County Sheriff's car as I drove in."

"We were hiking this morning and met up with the park ranger," Sam explained. "Not long after, the three of us discovered a dead woman. Looked like a tree limb fell on her."

"That's horrible."

"The ranger said she was a local hermit. He called her Bridget."

Stephen's face paled.

"You knew her?" I asked.

He nodded. "As well as anyone here did. We met not long after I contracted with the park for the apiary. I caught her checking one of my hives for honey a few weeks later." He slumped. "She's dead," he said quietly.

"And from what we saw, it wasn't an easy death," Sam added.

"What do you mean?"

"She had a severe head wound. The medical examiner will determine what actually killed her," Sam said.

"Do you know where she lived?" I asked.

Stephen shook his head. "There are lots of nooks and crannies around here somebody could live in if they wanted to." He glanced over his shoulder at a large canvas gym bag on the picnic table and then reached for it. "You two want to go with me to check my hives?"

"I will. Jamie?" Sam asked.

"The ranger's coming to talk to us in about an hour. Will it take longer than that?" I wasn't thrilled at the prospect of all those bees. As a scientist, I knew bees were crucial for pollination. Without them, we would have limited vegetables, fruits, and nuts to eat. Beekeepers played an essential role in managing bee populations, but still, visiting a beehive wasn't my idea of a great afternoon outing.

"He's coming here to talk to you? Why?" Stephen opened the bag and pulled out three white beekeeper's jackets, three netted hats and several pairs of thick white gloves.

"We were with the ranger who found the body," Sam said.

Stephen's hands dropped to his sides; his jaw tightened. "I don't want to get involved. I'll go check the apiary alone. You two take care of whatever with Snyder."

"Why would they involve you?" Sam asked. "You weren't there."

"The less contact I have with Roy Snyder and his people the better. I made my apiary contract with the former park manager. I don't need to give Roy any reason to deny my renewal. I can't lose this apiary. It's a fantastic honey source because of all the park's wildflower meadows." Stephen dug through the equipment he had laid on the table and returned two of the netted hats to the bag. "You know, honeybees are becoming harder and harder to find. They're disappearing. If it's not disease, it's overuse of high-powered pesticides."

"Can you tell us more about Bridget?" I interrupted. Stephen had done a smooth job of changing the subject. "I'm curious about her."

"Nothing to tell. She kept to herself." He ran his fingers through his black hair.

"But she stole your honey."

"She didn't steal it. I said she was checking the hive. Not the same thing. I'd better get to work." Stephen stuffed the remaining beekeeping equipment back into the duffle bag.

"But I'd like to go with you to check the hives," Sam said. "How long will it take?"

"Eight hives will take a couple of hours. I'd like to check for mites and disease. Need to add another super to each hive—this is prime honey production time—and I probably need to trim the grass." He frowned as he rubbed his forehead. "I don't see any way I can harvest any honey yet, although it's certainly there for the taking."

"A super?" Sam asked.

"Another framework layer inside the hive. The bees construct honeycomb on it. When there's no room to store the honey the bees make from the flower nectar, they swarm out of the hive to look for more space. Adding another level to the hive—a super—expands the hive so they don't move out."

I wished he were as eager to talk about Bridget as he was to explain beekeeping to us. I drummed my fingers on the picnic table, my head full of questions.

Sam glanced at me. "I've got hamburgers and hot dogs for a cookout. Can Cindy join us later?"

"Another time." Stephen zipped the bag closed.

"Let's at least sit down and catch up for a minute," Sam suggested.

I leaned against the picnic table, watching this exchange between the cousins. Abruptly, Stephen sighed, swung his leg over the picnic table bench, and sat down. "Okay." He folded his arms.

"I'll grab a couple of beers," I said.

"And I'll get some chips and salsa," Sam added as he followed me into the cabin. Once inside, Sam stopped and glanced through the screen door at his cousin.

"Is it my imagination, or is he upset about something?" I asked in my softest voice as I pulled a bowl from one of the cabinets.

Sam opened the refrigerator and grabbed three bottles of beer. "That's Stephen. He's always like that, especially if something isn't going the way he wants it to."

"I would like to see his beehive operation sometime." All I knew about beekeeping was that keepers wore lots of protective gear and that it was a good idea to calm the bees with smoke before messing with a hive.

"Hopefully, we can get him to take us to the apiary another day." Sam set the bottles on the counter and slid his arms around my waist. He kissed the tip of my nose.

A flush rose up on my neck and into my cheeks. My arms slid around him in a quick hug, and then we returned to the patio with beer, corn chips, and salsa.

"How is Cindy?" Sam asked. "I hope we see her while we're at the park."

Stephen's face darkened. He took the beer I offered, but stood up from the bench to lean against the table's edge. "She's okay. Can't promise you'll see her, though."

Sam and I waited, expecting more of an explanation about why his wife was unable to come see us, but Stephen lifted the bottle to his lips and chugged half the beer.

"Is your mom well?" Stephen asked Sam after he swallowed.

He and Sam talked about family members. I munched tortilla chips and salsa as they talked, and then returned to the refrigerator for another round of beer.

"Let's set up another time for you to come out while we're here," Sam said after the flow of stilted conversation ebbed.

"I'll get back to you about that." Stephen swallowed the remaining beer in his second bottle, then grabbed his gym bag.

As he started across the patio, one of the white state park trucks rumbled up the road and into the cul-de-sac. Stephen glanced at the truck and then turned back to Sam.

"Don't get too deeply involved in this investigation into Bridget's death. Believe me, it could get sticky." He hoisted the bag, slipping the handle over his shoulder as he rounded the corner of the stone cabin, and headed for his jeep.

Once Stephen was out of earshot, I said, "I don't know your cousin, but it seemed like something was bothering him."

"You're right. He was . . . *off*. Whatever it was, he didn't want to talk about it." He smiled teasingly. "But we're not going to let him ruin our good time this week, are we?"

I returned the smile, feeling my face light up.

CHAPTER 4

A few minutes later, Ranger Moyer knocked on the cabin's front door.

"I'll give you a ride down to the office," Moyer offered. "The park manager wants your statement for the sheriff."

The ranger had changed his shirt, but green stains on his pants told me that he had been on his knees in the undergrowth, probably helping with the lifting of the limb and the removal of Bridget's body.

Sam and I climbed onto the bench seat of the ranger's pickup to ride the few blocks through the manicured park to the office. Moyer kept the cab of his pickup clean and neat. The open ashtray held only a folded spearmint gum wrapper. An empty plastic convenience store cup sat in one side of the double cup holder. As he turned on the car, the radio blared. He flicked a knob, reducing the volume of Tim McGraw's voice from the airwaves. I was happy to listen to McGraw's hit song, "Something Like That." Sam slipped one arm around my shoulders.

A grassy area spotted with wooden picnic tables surrounded the one-story park office building. I stopped to read a large monument praising the Works Progress Administration program and the CCC workers who had constructed the park in the 1930s. Then I hurried to catch up with Sam. He waited at the office doorway, holding the old wooden screen door open.

Industrial gray carpet covered the floor of the reception area; plain white walls held only maps and tourism posters for decoration. Adjacent to the display, a door led into another part of the building.

"Hello," said a woman with black hair plaited into a waist-length braid. My nose traced the aroma of baking cookies to a dish of melted wax on a nearby table. We followed Doug past file cabinets and a central worktable, through a door, and into another small room where a gray-haired man sat reading at a worktable.

The man squinted up at Doug and pushed back in the chair. "Is it true? Is Bridget dead?" His bifocal lenses were perched on the end of a long beaked nose. Red splotches made up of tiny blood vessels marred his cheeks.

"I'm afraid so, Aiden. These folks and I found her this morning." The ranger nodded at us.

"Damn shame." The man shook his head as he glanced at Sam and me. "This park won't be the same without her," he added. Then he stood. "I'm Aiden Blunt."

Blunt gestured at the stacks of books and maps on the table. "I'm researching a book." He pulled off his glasses and rubbed at the reddish indentations in the flesh at the top of his nose.

"Aiden, Snyder's waiting to take their statements," the ranger said.

"Sure. Go ahead." The researcher waved us away, then sat down and turned the page of his book. He began to whistle an old tune that seemed very familiar.

"Maybe sometime you could tell me more about your research," I said.

Sam and the ranger moved to the doorway on the far side of the room. Voices from the nearby office erupted into an argument as I joined the others in a tiny hallway.

"You were disturbing evidence," a man—Snyder?—shouted.

"I was not. I didn't know she was dead," a woman yelled back.

A short-haired blonde in her late twenties burst from the room, dressed in a short-sleeved khaki shirt and blue jeans. She slammed into Doug, recovered, and glared up at him.

"Like I was intentionally 'disturbing' the evidence," she muttered before barreling past us.

Doug watched her storm away before he stepped into the cluttered office. File folders arranged in haphazard piles covered the desk. A small conference table in the corner was likewise covered with files and a copier. Three metal folding chairs had been shoved up to it. Another corner held a four-drawer filing cabinet with walkie-talkies and a radio transmitter/receiver on top. Tacks held overlapping maps onto the walls. The pervasive smell of cigarette smoke lingered in the air.

"Sir, here are the witnesses."

Snyder looked up at us and then shoved two papers across the one clean portion of his desk, followed by pens. "In your own words, write down what happened this morning both before and during your discovery of the body. The sheriff wants this information. He and his men are already out interviewing other park visitors."

Sam and I settled into the two chairs tucked up close to the front of the desk. We picked up the pens and filled out the forms. As we worked, Roy Snyder's chair creaked. Static on the radio and the sound of rustling paper broke the silence.

Sam slid his paper and pen back across the desk; I did the same. Once Snyder had both pages in front of him, the park manager checked off our contact numbers at the bottom of the page.

"This will do it. I understand you two are staying all week?"

"Yes. Cabin seven. After that, we'll be in Pawhuska, where we live." Sam tossed me a big smile. "We'd like copies of our statements, please."

The man glowered at Sam but stood up and used the copy machine on the conference table to make two copies. He handed them to us before he slid our statements into a folder. "The investigation should be simple enough. Old Bridget was in the wrong place at the wrong time. Who'd have thought a tree branch would take her down in the end? Too bad." He stood. "Thanks for coming in."

I blinked. We had seen the dried blood on Bridget's head, blood from a wound that must have occurred hours before the limb fell. The head wound had been serious, perhaps serious enough to kill her. Could she have been dead before the limb fell?

CHAPTER 5

"Sam, I don't think that tree branch killed Bridget," I said quietly as we crossed the road in front of the park office. We had declined the ranger's offer to drive us the short distance back to the cabin.

Sam took my hand, lacing my fingers with his own. "Maybe not. They'll get it sorted out, Jamie. That's their job."

Sam and I walked in silence. The sun glared down; heat rose up from the asphalt. So much for spring. An early summer had begun. A crow dive-bombed the road, grabbed something shiny with its beak, and flew back up to the trees.

"If she was murdered, will they shut down the park?"

Sam shrugged. "They'll conduct an investigation but keep the means of death under wraps. Most likely it won't even make the local newspapers."

"If it's up to Roy Snyder, it won't," I said. "I can't stop thinking about her. I want to know more about Bridget."

"And how are we going to find out?"

I sighed. What was it Stephen had said? 'Don't get involved.' Sam's cousin would tell us nothing. "I wish I knew."

We walked up the road. A squirrel dashed across in front of us and darted into the bushes, nearly colliding with a robin racing along a strip of lawn. The bird jabbed the earth with its beak, then ran a few feet further before stabbing at another spot. A cloudless blue sky hung above us, the perfect backdrop for the manicured park and the thick forest of native trees covering the nearby hills.

"'Secret Love'!" I cried.

"What?"

"That song Aiden was whistling. I remember it from the Lawrence Welk show my parents sometimes watched."

Sam's eyes questioned me.

"It's a silly Doris Day tune, popular in the fifties. Aiden must be about my mother's age."

Sam took my hand. "We need to have a song. 'Our song,' you know?"

I'd had such a song with my husband Ben—'Unforgettable'—but finding one for Sam and me had never crossed my mind. Our song, something that represented the way we felt about each other and the time we'd spent dating. I'd have to think about that.

Sam stopped and grinned at me. "How about 'She Drives Me Crazy' by the Fine Young Cannibals?"

I laughed, remembering the simple lyrics and the driving beat of the song, which had been popular in the early 1990s.

"It's appropriate," he insisted. "You do drive me crazy."

"Ditto, but that song is a decade old. Shouldn't our song be something current?"

"Maybe. Let's think about it. I bet we'll come up with something by the time we leave the park."

We walked on, both of us now thinking about music, about what our song could be.

At the cabin, Stephen's jeep was parked behind Sam's truck in the driveway. We rounded the corner of the cabin and found Stephen hunched over, head in his hands, on one of the picnic table benches. He vaulted to his feet as we neared.

"Damn coons got into two of my hives. I need your help, Sam."

"What can I do?"

"Help me put the hives back together and set up something to scare those bandits away for good. Otherwise, I'll have to move the entire apiary." He clenched his teeth and twisted his ball cap. "No telling how many bees died when the hive over-turned." He grimaced at Sam.

"Jamie? You want to go?" Sam asked.

I shook my head. "I'd be in the way. I might give my mom a call. Maybe I can get her to tell me some stories about growing up around here."

"Good luck with that," Sam said.

He kissed me, and then the two men trotted toward Stephen's vehicle. Sam stuck his hand out the window and waved as the jeep zoomed off down the blacktop road.

In the kitchen, I retrieved a paper sack and then returned to the patio to pick up the empty bottles of beer. I'd have to find out where the recycling depot was located in my new hometown.

The tune Aiden Blunt had been whistling played in my mind, along with the words: *Once I had a secret love . . .*

"Hello," someone called. I dropped the last bottle into the sack and swiveled around. The young blond woman Sam and I had seen in the office strode toward me across the wide lawn separating our cabin from those on the other loop of the cabin complex.

"Hi." I shaded my eyes from the fierce sunlight.

"I'm Celeste, the park's summer naturalist. Have you had a chance to do much hiking in the park yet?" she asked. The young woman, who was a few inches shorter than I, had sapphire eyes and a wide smile that showed straight white teeth.

"We hiked the Creek Loop Trail this morning. My fiancé and I are staying for the week, so we'll have time to hike most of the park's trails while we're here. I'm Jamie."

"Great! Fiancé? When's the wedding?" She leaned against the end of the picnic table and folded her arms.

"Not sure when or where. We'll talk about it this week." A bubble of excitement played in my stomach. The fact that I was marrying Sam still didn't feel quite real.

She glanced toward the line of trees a few yards away and smiled again. "I lead a group hike on Saturday mornings. We'll gather tomorrow at the park office about eight if you'd like to join us." She tucked her short blond hair behind her ears and scanned the other nearby cabins. "Something else you might be interested in . . . There will be a program Sunday night in the group camp dining hall. We have a guest speaker, a local man who's doing research for a book about the CCC camps and the state park projects."

"I think we met him earlier. Aiden? Is he the speaker?"

"Yes." She eyed me closely. "You were at the park office this morning, weren't you? You and your fiancé were with Doug when he found Bridget."

Her look shifted away from me; she stared into space. "I feel bad about that. We all do."

"I understand Bridget lived in the park."

"Yes, for years, I think. She probably knew more about the animals and plants here than anyone. Certainly more than Snyder."

"Do you know why she lived out here?" I couldn't subdue my curiosity about the hermit's background. It had hardly left my thoughts since we'd found her body.

"Bridget didn't talk about it. She kept to herself most of the time. Found food in the forest. Raised a few vegetables in a little clearing. Made her own soaps and candles from beeswax. Bridget knew how to treat a snake bite or bee sting and what to put on a poison ivy rash."

Celeste had known and admired the hermit. She probably knew where the woman had lived. Earlier today, Snyder had said Celeste had been 'disturbing the evidence.' Where?

"I'd love to stay and chat, but I can't." Celeste straightened and moved away from the picnic table. "I need to pass the word on to these other people about the walk tomorrow morning and the program. I'm sure I'll see you again, Jamie." The naturalist headed for the cabin next door.

I was tempted to follow and ply her with questions, to make her talk to me, but I didn't. As she meandered across the lawn, a maintenance employee who'd been working around the trees in the yard of an adjacent cabin turned off his grass trimmer. He watched Celeste as she talked with the elderly couple next door. When she moved on a few minutes later, he turned on the trimmer again. Although Celeste seemed to look right at him, she didn't smile.

I leaned back in a canvas camp chair we'd brought with us, closed my eyes, and let the sun wash over me. Celeste knew Bridget. Could I get her to tell me the woman's history? Bridget had survival skills, but I still couldn't wrap my head around the fact she had chosen to live out here alone.

"How are the bees?" I asked a few minutes later, when Sam and Stephen stepped into the cabin. I had moved from the patio to the kitchen and was at work shaping patties of ground beef into hamburgers and storing them in a wax paper-lined plastic container. We'd use the meat for several meals while we were at the cabin, either as burgers or reshaped into meatballs or a meatloaf. I'd already finished preparing a similar container of marinated and seasoned chicken breasts and was anticipating a week of cooking outside on the grill.

Sam reached into the refrigerator for a bottle of water and handed a second bottle to Stephen. "The coons made a mess of two of the hives. We put them back together."

"The worst thing is that I couldn't find one hive's queen. I hope she wasn't injured," Stephen grumbled.

In spite of his obvious concern about the queen bee, Stephen appeared to be less anxious than he had been this morning.

"How can you actually 'find' a queen bee in the middle of a hive full of bees?" I asked.

"The queen has a different shape. Much bigger overall with a huge abdomen. But that doesn't make her easy to find," Stephen said. "She spends all day laying eggs. When there is no more space for eggs, or if something disturbs the hive, she is likely to gather her bees and fly away to find a new place to live."

"Do all of the bees follow her when she flies away?"

"Yes. They swarm. You've heard of people who discover a huge number of bees in a tree in their yard or in the wall of their house? That's a swarm. Some bee professionals specialize in capturing swarms and relocating them. I've never had to try." Stephen chugged the bottle of water and set the empty on the counter.

He was much more open—friendly, even—and I grabbed at the chance to keep him talking, maybe even to get him to talk about Bridget. "When did you get interested in beekeeping?"

"My father kept bee boxes on our farm when I was a kid so they would pollinate the vegetables. I grew up helping him."

"I think it's great the park allows you to keep an apiary here. How did it come about?"

"There were hives here that needed to be tended. The park superintendent knew I was a keeper. It was in the spring. March, I think. The other beekeeper was sick and unable to tend the hives at a critical time. The hives were in danger of losing their queens once the flowers bloomed and honey production began again. I stepped in to help out."

"And the recluse we found this morning knew something about keeping bees?"

"Most beekeepers follow the same basic methodology. Bridget was self-taught. I learned from my father." He glanced at Sam. "You remember him, don't you? Very precise and by-the-book. Things Bridget was not."

I put the last of the meat into the refrigerator and turned to stir the pot of stew simmering on the stove. "Can you stay for dinner? It's almost ready."

"Cindy will be waiting. She didn't expect me to be gone this long," Stephen said, checking his watch. "I should go. We'll do it another time."

After Stephen's truck had chugged away down the street, Sam sat at the tiny kitchen table and watched as I pulled out plates and bowls for the stew.

"It was an interesting afternoon," he said. "Beekeeping is a lot of work. But you couldn't pay me enough to do it without one of those beekeeper suits and a netted hat on. At one point, dozens of bees crawled on Stephen's arm. He expanded the honey-making capacity of the hives with supers. He used large specialized tongs to insert them once the lid was off the hive."

"I'm impressed," I said, leaning back against the sink. "Over the course of the afternoon, did Stephen say anything more about Cindy? Or Bridget?"

"No. And I didn't ask. If you hadn't noticed, he can be very close-mouthed when he chooses to be."

"Hm," I said, smiling at my fiancé. "Must run in the family."

Sam smirked but let my little jab go without comment. He knew it was true. Most people only shared what had to be shared about themselves and their family members.

We all keep secrets, even from those we love the most.

CHAPTER 6

Saturday, May 18

"We can do our own nature walk," Sam grumbled on Saturday morning. "I don't want to get caught up in a slow-moving group. I hike for the exercise." He nuzzled my neck.

"I do, too," I said as I rolled out of the bed. "But we'll learn more if we take the guided hike. We have all week to wander around on our own. Get up, sweetheart."

I left the bedroom and stepped into the bathroom's small shower. He had no idea how tempted I was to forget the walk and stay in bed. For months, I had been craving time with him, and our alone time last night had been everything I'd wanted it to be. Sam's lovemaking had been slow and sensuous. Now, my body tingled both from the sweet memories of last night and the sharp needles of water from the shower spray.

The aroma of cooking bacon wafted into the bathroom. He'd gotten up and was cooking breakfast. Was there anything not to like about this man of mine?

I strapped my fanny pack around my waist and scooted it so that the little pouch hung in front and within easy reach. Inside, I had my compass, matches in a round water-proof cylinder, a tiny plastic bag of cotton balls, a pack of tissues, and a pocket mirror. My pack also contained a folding camping tool that included pliers, a knife, and scissors. It was a standing joke with my kids that I was over-prepared for a hike around the block. I flicked on the little flashlight to be sure it didn't need a battery replacement.

"What do you think that naturalist is going to tell you that you don't already know?" Sam asked when I tromped into the kitchen in my hiking boots. "Both of us know a lot about Oklahoma plants and animals. Between your aunt and my family, we've learned all about ecosystems: what animal eats what, what their habitat requirements are, nocturnal or diurnal . . ."

"I'm not arguing with you." I slid my arms around him and hugged his back. "If you don't want to go, stay here. I think it'll be interesting. I need to get my mind off that poor hermit woman."

Slowly, Sam's frown broke into a smile. "Okay. I've registered my complaint. Can we peel off from the group at some point if it goes on too long?" He slid pancakes off the griddle and onto plates, then added strips of bacon before setting the plates on the table.

"Sure." I slathered butter on my pancakes and drowned them in maple syrup.

Sam dropped into his chair and did the same with his food. "Eat fast or we're going to be late."

Both the older couple and the young family that I had watched unpack the previous evening were waiting outside the park office with Celeste, the naturalist I had met yesterday afternoon. She checked her watch as we neared, then motioned for all of us to come close. A middle-aged couple hurried down the road from the RV park and joined our group.

"Good morning," Celeste said. "Great to have you all join me at Osage Hills for the Saturday nature walk. I'm Celeste, the seasonal naturalist."

"Hi, Celeste." A little boy, the youngest member of the family who had moved into the cabin across from ours, spoke up, then immediately ducked his head and buried his face in his father's leg.

"I'd like each of you to tell the group your name and where you are from before we begin our walk," Celeste said.

"We're Bernard and Betty Wood from Wichita, Kansas," the oldest member of the group said. The man, who was probably close to my mother's age, was bald except for a band of white hair that circled his head from ear to ear. His wife was at least a foot shorter than he and had a head of fluffy too-black hair. They held hands. This was the pair I'd seen bustling around the cabin next door yesterday afternoon.

"We're Jason and Crystal Hargis, and our kids Emma and Jacob from Tulsa," the mother of the family said when she introduced her group. Her husband frowned at the kids, who were chasing each other around him, trying to pinch one another.

"Sam Mazie and Jamie Aldrich, from Pawhuska," Sam said. "Soon to be Jamie Mazie." He grinned; blood rushed to my face. The Woods clapped.

"Suzanne and Michael Cooper from Oklahoma City," the middle-aged woman from the RV camp said. The Coopers were both tall and thin, fully outfitted from L.L. Bean with hiking boots, trousers, and long-sleeved button shirts designed for outdoor activities.

"Great group! Feel free to ask questions at any point throughout the walk. The topic today is Oklahoma flora and fauna, with a little bit of history thrown in here and there." Celeste headed off down the main road and we all followed. We passed the cabin turnoff and turned onto another road marked with a sign that read *Swimming Pool.*

Sam and I trailed behind the group. About every twenty yards, Celeste would stop, wait for everyone to clump together, and then recite a fact about something we'd passed on the trail or were standing near. Soon, I was afraid Sam was correct. The information might be new and interesting to several members of the group, but not to me or Sam.

We stepped off the road and onto a lawn that stretched between the paved road and the creek. A large, old stone-and-log picnic shelter stood on the far side of the lawn. Rock cliffs towered behind the shelter. Between the cliffs and the shelter, a line of thick trees shadowed the meandering stream.

"This is Shelter 2, the largest and most enduring structure built by the CCC here at Osage Hills," Celeste explained. "The camp was occupied by Company 895 and included 189 young men between the ages of 18 and 23. They worked here constructing the park until 1941, building the roads and trails, clearing picnic and lawn areas. They also assembled cabins, this picnic shelter, and the community center at the group camp. When they first arrived, they had to finish their own camp facilities, which had been started by a team of local carpenters and laborers."

"Did they get paid to work here?" Jacob asked. "Or was it like a prison camp?"

"Yes, they were paid to work here." Celeste smiled at the boy. "That was the whole purpose of that government program, to provide employment for young men who couldn't find work during the time known as the Great Depression in the 1930s."

"How much did they get paid?" Jacob asked.

"$30 a month," Celeste answered. "Doesn't seem like much now, but it was a lot at that time. The young men, who were selected for the program because they were unable to find work and had families they needed to support, were required to send $25 of that money home to their parents."

"Can we see where they lived?" Emma asked.

"There's not much left. A nature trail north of the tent camping area winds through the site on the way to the lake. All of the buildings were completely dismantled when the camp closed down in 1941. You can see a big stone fireplace and some foundations and concrete pads that supported two water towers. That's about all."

A few yards ahead, signage identified the start of the nature trail that led to the waterfalls and Sand Creek. As we walked along the wide, sandy trail, Celeste pointed out scat—the drop-pings of mammals—tree rubbings, worm castings, and raccoon tracks. The two kids alternated between shouting, "Cool!" and "Gross!" depending on what fact Celeste was sharing.

Following a short hike through the trees, the group of us stood above the banks of Sand Creek. "Okay, everyone gather close in," Celeste instructed. Water roared beyond the thick foliage of cottonwoods and willows. "It's steep here in this washout; be careful going down to the water. We're now at the Falls; the most popular picnic and hiking area in the park. We'll make our way down this washout to the river bank, where we'll find flat rocks, small trees and lots of brush. Sand Creek is just beyond. Take a few minutes to explore, then join me by the big dead tree that you'll see leaning from the bank toward the creek."

Celeste led the way down to the rock-strewn shore of the swiftly flowing water. The creek tumbled over the rocks, swirling in pools and foaming on its way downstream.

Jacob and Emma immediately skipped toward the edge of the water, and the other members of the group took photos at the picturesque spot. A blue heron lifted up from the edge of the creek and flapped away. The musky scent of cottonwoods and the sweet perfume of flowering shrubs hung in the air.

"Dad! Over here! See what I found!" Jacob Hargis shouted.

His father Jason quickly crossed the rocks to where the ten-year-old stood, pointing down at one of the pools. Sam and I stepped over to see what had the boy so excited.

His father plucked an object from the water. "It's an old coin. All crusted up." The man examined this clear pool and others nearby in the sandstone, which stretched across the wide creek. "Wonder if there are any more around here."

Celeste made her way to where we stood by the water. Mike Cooper trekked across the rocks behind her.

Jason held out the coin. "My son Jacob found this. Can we keep it?"

Celeste took the coin and examined it. "Looks old—might

be worth something. The waterfalls here have been a popular picnic spot forever. No telling how long the coin has been in the river. All these recent rains have uncovered it." She adjusted her small backpack. "Keep it if you want." She handed the coin to Jason. "Okay, let's reconvene over there," she called, pointing toward a dead tree.

Mike Cooper, Jason, and Jacob started off across the rocks, stepping carefully over mud pools, small shrubs, and wide cracks between the flat stones. Jason handed the coin to his son, who tucked it into his backpack.

The naturalist marched away to wait for the others by the tree.

Instead of joining them, Sam and I split off at the washout where we had climbed down to the stream. We eased back up onto the trail and retraced our steps to the trailhead near the park's swimming pool. Sam and I hiked north along the road, eventually passing the cabin loop.

"We're headed for the lake," I said.

"Yeah, and the old CCC camp."

I rolled up the sleeves of my denim shirt. "Okay. Now is as good a time as any for a long hike. Let's do it before it gets any hotter." I pulled my hair back into a ponytail, securing it with an elastic band I pulled from my fanny pack.

"I want to get a feel for that camp." Sam scanned the blue sky for clouds, watching for signs of a possible rain shower. As far as we could see, the sky held only a depth of blue. "Stephen agreed with Celeste: there's not much left. We'll need to watch out for a few basements and a cistern or two if we explore more than the perimeter where the Tourism Department posted signage. He told me that trees, underbrush, and grass have grown throughout the open area where the camp once was. It's not too far from the meadow where his apiary is."

"And how do you know that?" I asked.

"I asked him. And for once, he gave me a straight answer."

CHAPTER 7

Sam and I picked our way through the tall grass clumps and small bushes that now covered the former CCC camp. We had walked a mile or so down the park's main asphalt road and then followed the trail that skirted the west edge of Lake Lookout. On the north end of the lake, we had taken a south-westerly turn to pass through the old site. Now, other than occasional concrete steps leading nowhere or foundations that framed basements, little evidence of the barracks or other buildings at the camp remained. Sam and I stopped beside an enormous towering chimney, which the map identified as having once been part of the officer's quarters.

"It's a little hard to imagine all the activity that took place here in the thirties," Sam said. "There's nothing left."

As we walked through grass, greening weeds, and forest debris, a shadow passed over us. A turkey vulture soared through the tree canopy, then circled again.

"Sam, look."

The bird perched in a tree and stared down at us. Seconds later, another vulture flapped its way to the tree and settled onto an adjacent branch.

"They smell something dead," Sam said.

I sniffed the air. "Probably nothing. A rabbit or raccoon. Leftovers from a coyote's breakfast."

"I wouldn't think much of it, but after yesterday . . . Let's have a look around."

We crossed a sunny opening and walked back into shadows and thicker trees, searching the ground for whatever the vultures were waiting to eat. I brushed away a fly that buzzed at my face. A spot on the back of my neck began to itch. I couldn't smell anything but growing plants and fertile earth, but I didn't have the heightened sense of smell with which a vulture–or any bird of prey–was gifted.

Sam walked toward the far side of the camp ruins, where foundations and steps broke the even line of the earth. "Over here, Jamie," he called.

The tone of his voice alerted me that he had found something; I cautiously moved in his direction. A sparkling sunbeam caught the silken web of a spider, and I ducked. My throat tightened. The possibility of walking into a cobweb and ending up with spiders in my hair sent chills up my spine. Memories fluttered of a tunnel, of cobwebs sticking to my face, my hair, my neck. This was not a place where I wanted to linger.

When I finally drew close enough to see Sam's face, I knew he'd found whatever the vultures were here for. I glanced down at a rectangular opening in the ground. Dark water stood a foot deep or more in what was now an open, cement-sided pool, probably the camp's water cistern. Twigs and debris floated around the bloated body of a deer.

"Um. I'll contact the park office," Sam said in a low voice. "They'll want to get this out of here."

The vultures flapped their wings.

The world around me began to spin. "I gotta move back," I muttered. I took a step and fell to my knees.

Sam grabbed my arm. "Honey? Are you okay?"

"Give me a minute." I focused on an acorn on the ground in front of me and waited for the spinning to stop.

Sam and I moved away from the cistern, across an open space and into the shade of a scraggly half-dead elm tree.

"I've had enough of bodies, and it's getting hot." I wiped my forehead. "Will that trail lead us back to the cabins? It might be cooler than the asphalt road."

Sam pulled the park map from the pocket of his shorts and studied the trail system. "I think so, and we'll see another part of the park."

"Let's do it."

After taking long swigs from the water bottles we carried, we found the trail's entrance and ducked back into the shade of the forest. Here, the trail was wide and rocky. Dappled sunlight created patterns of light on the thick undergrowth. Sam forged ahead, striding along the path. I hurried to keep up.

We turned south and entered a heavily wooded section where little light penetrated to the forest floor. Vines snaked up the oak tree trunks and across the ground, covering small bushes and baby trees completely.

"What's that over there?" Sam asked. I followed his look to an old stone wall twenty feet off the trail.

"A building?" I scanned the area and saw what could have been an adjoining wall, also covered with vegetation. "Or just a wall marking someone's property. Let's check it out."

I stopped to study a white shelf fungus growing on an aged post oak tree and then followed Sam. We shoved through bushes and small trees, avoiding a stand of sumac, and reached the wall. Created by stacking worn sandstone rocks, it looked much older than the CCC structures we had seen elsewhere in the park. Vines crawled across many sections, but here and there, entire rocks had been exposed to the elements. Over the years, many of them had been carved with names and initials.

Sam moved along the rock, touching the stones, pushing aside ivy, and bending to get a closer look.

"Jamie. Your mother's name was Jamison, right?"

"Yes. Mary Jamison. She grew up about twenty miles from here."

"Check this out."

He pulled a strand of ivy away from the rock. In letters now deeply worn, someone had carved, "Patrick Gallagher loves Mary Jamison. 1954."

"Your mom and dad?" Sam asked.

"I don't know anyone named Patrick Gallagher." An electric shock tingled down my back.

"But she could have been here at the park. It's close to her home. When did she and your dad get married?"

"1955."

"An earlier boyfriend, maybe?"

"Could have been." But one mother had not talked about. It was another example of the secrecy that cloaked my mother's early life and left me feeling like an outsider in her eyes.

Sam let the ivy drop back over the stones and moved farther down along the wall.

I lingered at the place he had found my mother's name. She had never shared any memories of childhood or teenage years. And she probably did date before she met my father. But this sounded serious. Patrick Gallagher had *loved* her. Who was he?

CHAPTER 8

Once again, Stephen's truck was sitting in the driveway when we returned to the cabin. But this time, there was no sign of him anywhere.

"Do you think we're going to see a lot of Stephen while we're here?" I asked.

Sam's expression was doubtful. "He's usually not very social."

He headed around to the back of the cabin while I went inside, eager to change out of my hiking clothes and into a tank top and shorts. The midday sun beat down.

When I stepped out onto the back patio a few minutes later, Sam sat at the picnic table, alone.

"No Stephen?"

"Wonder where he went." Sam studied the tree line a few yards away from our patio.

"Maybe he went for a little walk since we weren't here."

A flash of color shone through the trees, and Stephen stepped out of the forest and off the nature trail close to the cabins.

"You two been out hiking again today?" he called.

"Yes, and so have you," Sam said.

Stephen glanced back at the trees. "It's been a while since I've used these trails. For the most part, I'm at the apiary." He slipped a backpack off his shoulder and set it on the ground. "I decided to take a walk, hoping you'd be back when I returned."

"See anything interesting?" Sam asked.

"Not really. Did you?"

Sam smiled at me. I saw no reason to share the inscription on the wall with Stephen. "We took the morning nature walk with the park naturalist and then walked up to the old CCC camp."

"Did you go by the apiary?"

"No. Took the forest trail back here. It seemed direct on the map, but it was rocky in places and harder to navigate than I expected. Is that where you've been?"

"Earlier. I worked around the hives an hour or so. Actually, I came here and ate a sandwich on your picnic table. Nice shady spot." His brow wrinkled. "I'll get out of your hair."

"Stephen, you never said what you wanted." Sam followed his cousin to the corner of the cabin.

"Nothing important. Checking on you, that's all," he called over his shoulder.

Thirty minutes later, I carried one of our folding camp chairs away from the cabin to the shade made by a duo of blackjacks surrounded by the cabin's back lawn. Sam had taken the truck and driven into Bartlesville to get a few more supplies for our stay and to pick up Queenie. Sam's basset-mix pooch was keeping my cousin Trudy company in Pawhuska while we were at the park, but she had agreed to let the dog spend the two weekend nights with us as long as we returned her Monday.

A powerful engine roared in front of the cabin. It didn't sound like Sam's truck or Stephen's jeep. The ranger again? I stepped inside and headed to the door.

When I pulled the door open, Sheriff John Standingbear glanced first at me, then behind me into the living room.

"Sam here? I'm John Standingbear. We met yesterday."

"I remember, Sheriff. I'm Jamie, Sam's fiancée. We weren't introduced."

"No. It wasn't a good time for meeting new people. That's one of the reasons I wanted to stop by. I wanted to meet the lady who convinced Sam life was worth living after all. He had a tough time when Reba passed away." His soft eyes held sympathy and kindness.

"He was still having a tough time when we met last spring. He's better now."

"I can see why." The man smiled, revealing strong, straight white teeth. Instead of a stern law enforcement official, he was a pleasant, mature good-looking man. "And a woman who still blushes. Sam is a lucky man."

I turned away. "Come on in, Sheriff. Sam should be back from Bartlesville shortly."

"Oh, I can't stay. I have something to ask you. Yesterday morning, did you see or hear anything you didn't mention on your statement?" His face settled back into that of the stern sheriff.

"I think we put everything on our statement. I know I mentioned the scream that drew us there."

The sheriff squinted at me. "Yes. You, Sam, and Ranger Moyer all mentioned the scream." He blew his breath out. "But I have to tell you something. The ME's preliminary report indicates that when Bridget was found, she'd been dead for several hours. It wasn't Bridget who screamed."

"We didn't see anyone else there."

"Someone else was there, but they weren't responsible for her death. Probably, the head wound killed her," the sheriff said.

The image flashed into my head. Dried blood in her matted hair, and staring eyes.

"I saw a couple of cougar tracks, partials on the trail not too far from the body. Did you notice them?" Standingbear asked.

A cougar? I knew the big cats roamed throughout most of the United States, but I'd never considered the fact they might live here, on the border between prairie and forest. "I didn't."

"Be aware. They are solitary and nocturnal for the most part. Seldom seen." He watched a fly land on his shirtsleeve, do a quickstep, and then buzz away. "Speaking of tracks, I would like to take an imprint of the shoes you were wearing. So we can identify your prints among those we found on site. Sometimes unusual forensic evidence turns up."

"Let me get them for you." I left the room, grabbed my boots from the bedroom closet, and returned to the front door. I handed him the lightweight hiking boots I'd been wearing both yesterday and this morning.

"And Sam's shoes, too. If he's not wearing them . . ."

"I'm afraid he is. Can you stop back by later?"

"It may be tomorrow." He stepped out onto the porch and picked up a bag of white powder he had apparently brought with him. "Give me a second. I can make the cast here. If I could trouble you for a little water . . ." He showed me a mark on the side of the bag that indicated the water line. I carried the bag into the kitchen and filled it.

By the time I returned, he had taken my shoes to a spot of bare dirt next to the driveway and made a deep impression of the sole of one shoe in the soft earth. I handed him the bag of plaster and took back my shoes.

"I'll make the print now and be back to pick it up in about forty-five minutes. I have several more prints to make." He kneaded the bag several times with his hands before pouring the batter-like liquid over the track, filling each shoeprint and extending the casting several inches to each side of the shoe. "Perfect." He wadded up the sack and stepped back from the cast. "Thanks for your time, Jamie. It's nice to see you. Tell Sam I'll catch up with him another time. Soon, I hope."

John Standingbear walked to his SUV. I glanced at the hardening cast of my shoeprint before I traipsed back through the cabin and outside to once again sit in the yard.

A light breeze tickled my skin; I shivered and turned in the chair so that I faced the sun's rays. If I could warm up and settle my mind, I might be able to take a nap. I pushed Bridget's image as far back in my brain as I could and concentrated on the sun warming my body and the puffy clouds drifting across the sky.

So I told a friendly star, the way that dreamers often do . . . The words of the Doris Day song came to me as soon as I closed my eyes. My mind zipped from the song to yesterday's grisly discovery. I pushed the picture of Bridget's face out of my mind and thought of the wall inscription with my mother's name. I owed her a phone call anyway. Now was as good a time as any.

As far as I knew, no one, not even my sister Ellen, had ever had any success at probing Mother's past. Even after I had discovered my great aunt's family secrets during a visit to Pawhuska a year ago, Mother had refused to talk about her family's history. If she would not discuss ancestors long dead, I knew she would refuse to talk about the personal escapades of her youth.

How was she going to respond when I asked her about this inscription? I was determined to learn about her romance with Gallagher. This little tidbit, so small in the scheme of things, was an opportunity for her to share one of her secrets with me. A grin worked its way onto my face as I set up a camp chair on the back patio. I punched her number in on my cell phone.

She picked up on the second ring.

"Mother, how are you?"

"As good as can be expected. Where are you?" She sounded irritated.

"In Oklahoma. Planning my future with Sam."

"Oh."

Her single-word response made me determined to get to the reason I had called. I knew she didn't want me to move to Oklahoma; she wanted Sam to move to New Mexico. But that wasn't happening. It was much easier for me to find a teaching position in another state than it was for Sam to start up an entire new family law practice.

"Sam and I are taking a few days to relax. We're over at Osage Hills State Park, between Bartlesville and Pawhuska. You remember it?"

"Don't think so. Parks weren't exactly a place my family frequented. We were too busy working the farm." She didn't miss a beat.

"Oh, I'm sure you came to this park. It's not far from where you lived."

"Why are you insisting?" she demanded, now even more irritated.

"Because I found your name carved into a sandstone wall, and the date, 1954." I couldn't help but laugh a little as I explained. "The inscription says, 'Patrick Gallagher loves Mary Jameson, 1954.' Who was he, Mother?"

"Oh, dear," she whispered.

She would be frowning into the phone, her forehead furrowed and her fingers working at a short lock of hair in front of her ear. For a few seconds, I felt bad about ambushing her with this information.

"Mother, big deal if you had a boyfriend before you married Dad. Who cares now? How did you meet Patrick?"

"I would rather not talk about it," she muttered.

"But I'd like to know. It's part of your past, and you've never told me anything." My voice sounded whiny.

"He was a friend. Back before I met your dad." She cleared her throat. "I was at that park for church Bible camp."

"So, were you both summer campers?" Patrick had gone to a lot of work to carve his love inscription. It couldn't have been just a summer fling.

Mother cleared her throat again. "This is silly. I don't want to talk about it."

"Mom, it's not a big deal. Just share it with me," I pleaded. "Please."

She sighed and then blew out her breath. "He was a counselor like I was, but from another church. We spent some time together."

"He carved 'Patrick loves Mary.' Did you feel the same?"

"Jamie Lynne, this is none of your business," she huffed.

I chuckled to myself. She had resorted to using my middle name so I wouldn't ask any more questions. This tactic no longer worked on her forty-plus-year-old daughter.

"Oh, come on, why not tell me all about it?"

She let out an exasperated sigh. "I didn't love him. He loved me. Summer camp ended. I never saw him again. Why are you and Sam at that park? There can't be much to do there."

"Sam and I are exploring and talking about our future. This park has an interesting past, with the CCC construction and all."

"I remember," Mother said softly.

"But we also stumbled into something. We found a dead woman yesterday morning."

Mother gasped. "How awful. Why are you still there?"

"The person who died lived in the park. She was a hermit. Her name was Bridget."

"B– B– Bridget?" Mother breathed. She coughed and cleared her throat. "Time to, ah, take my medicine. And get my nap. We'll talk later."

The phone clicked in my ear. I closed my eyes and sank back into the canvas folding chair, letting the afternoon breeze ruffle my hair. Now I had more questions than before. Mother had known Patrick Gallagher. And she had reacted to Bridget's name. Had she known the hermit?

I wanted to call her back, but most likely, this was all the information I would get out of her today. And I should count myself lucky to have had her open up as much as she did. Tonight, she would think about Patrick and Bridget. Tomorrow, she might be even more willing to talk.

I remembered often overhearing my Dad allude to something that had happened when he and my mother were young. He would be teasing, trying to lighten her mood, to get her to smile. My mother would shush him. "The past is gone. I won't talk about it," she would say under her breath. Sometimes she locked herself in the bathroom afterwards.

But there were other ways to find information about Patrick Gallagher. Bartlesville was only a short drive away. The family history section of the city library would have records of both Patrick's family and my mother's since they were residents of the area. If I wanted info about the church camp, the park might have archives with records of the group camp's usage. They might go back to the summer of 1954.

Bridget. Who was she? Mother had grown up here. She had gone to camp here. I felt certain my mother had known her.

I eased back into the chair and soaked up the spring afternoon sun. The elderly couple who occupied the cabin next door puttered around the patio, traipsing in and out of the cabin. On the other side of the narrow asphalt road, a family unloaded supplies as they turned the cabin into their weekend getaway. Behind me, on the lawn, a maintenance worker used a gas-powered weed eater to trim grass around scattered trees and bushes.

I focused on my mother. Why had Patrick taken the time to carve that inscription if my mother didn't feel the same? Why had the relationship ended? Was it because she met my father?

My imagination darted to unexpected places. Had my mother had a sexual relationship *before* my father? It didn't seem possible. Then again, my mother had to have had the usual sexual cravings of a blossoming teenage girl. She couldn't have always been as buttoned up as she was now.

Inside the cabin, my cell phone rang. I made a mad dash into the cabin, grabbed the phone from my purse, and punched it on.

"Boy, have you done it this time." My sister Ellen didn't even wait until I'd said hello to begin her usual tirade. "Mom is really upset."

"What else is new?" It wasn't unusual for my mother to

become upset after talking to me. She'd been doing it for over forty years now. "What did I do this time?" Even as I asked the question, I already knew. Patrick Gallagher, for one. And Bridget, the hermit, for two. I carried the phone with me back out onto the small patio and my seat in the sun.

"You know Mother always says the past is the past. Leave it alone. It was bad enough that you had to dig into all of that family history about Pawhuska and the Osages last year. But now . . . Truthfully, I've never seen her so upset. I just left there. I'd stopped by to drop off some issues of the *New Mexico Magazine*. She'd just gotten off the phone with you, hadn't she?"

The heavy silence Ellen fell into was an opportunity for me to confess and ask forgiveness. Instead, I wondered why a conversation about someone my mother had left behind fifty years ago and a simple statement that a hermit had died in the park could have upset my mother this much.

"Well? Didn't you realize you were going to upset her?" Ellen prodded.

"Ellen, Mother grew up in this area. Sam and I found her name carved into a stone wall here at the park, along with a man's name. How could I not ask about that? Obviously, it's an old boyfriend. I'm curious, that's all." I closed my eyes and let the hot sun seep into my skin.

"An old boyfriend she has never said a word about." Ellen was using her best lecturing voice. "Doesn't that give you some clue that he isn't important to her?"

"No. It doesn't. If I believed that, very little is important to our mother. She never talks about her past. It's like she dropped in from a faraway galaxy right before she met Dad and got married. It's ridiculous." I straightened and perched on the end of the chair seat.

"She is entitled to her privacy."

"We went through all of this last year. Do you think Mother was entitled to keep our heritage from us, or to bury the family's enormous tragedy?" I stood up.

She snorted. "Your discovery of Elizabeth's secret has not changed anything in my daily life. And as far as our heritage, I can't see that it matters much. As Mother says, the past is in the past. She and I both wish you could get that through your head."

My temper boiled. This conversation was a repeat of conversations we'd had before. Ellen would not listen to anything I said, and I felt the same about what she said. Every time this happened, I vowed not to let her get under my skin. But she did.

"To change the subject, how's Randy? Have you been to the veterans home this week?" I asked. My older brother was never far from my thoughts, and although I had stopped by to see him on Tuesday, before I headed for Oklahoma, I wanted an update. His condition changed daily. On Tuesday, he'd been uncertain who I was, but he'd hugged me and cried when I left all the same.

"Oh, no you don't. We're not finished with this conversation about Mother. I want you to promise me you won't bring this man's name up again. Patrick whoever. Promise?"

"You know I can't promise that."

"Please. And about Randy. He's had a bad week. The PTSD meds calm him down, but the dosage is wrong, I think. He's like a zombie. I plan to talk to Dr. Stanton tomorrow. And it might help if you gave the doctor a call, too. Do you have his number? It's going to be hard on Randy not to see you regularly. Last summer, while you stayed in Oklahoma with Elizabeth, he was especially agitated. And I can see it beginning all over again."

I sat back in the chair. *Here we go again. Do all families do this?* In my family, guilt was like a badminton birdie, knocked back and forth to me from across the net, where my mother and sister doubled-teamed me.

CHAPTER 9

A dog barked. Although I'd been dozing in the shade, I was instantly awake. I knew that bark.

"Queenie!" I called. The low-slung dog rounded the corner of the cabin, her long, soft ears flapping against her head. She smiled a doggy smile and charged at me, thudding into my legs, licking at my hands and talking in her happy dog voice.

"Nice reunion," Sam said. He held two grocery sacks in his arms, so I bolted from the chair and flew across the patio to open the back door for him.

"I'm glad to see you both." I stooped to pet the dog, rubbing her ears and scratching between her shoulder blades. "Need help with more bags?"

"Nope. Just one more. I'll get it. You girls get reacquainted. After all, it's been a whole forty-eight hours since we left Pawhuska."

I scratched more of Queenie's favorite spots: behind her ears, above her long spike of a tail, and on her breastbone. She fastened her bright brown eyes on me with doggy love and grunted as I scratched.

When Sam had deposited the supplies in the kitchen, he returned to the patio and handed me a flier. "This was clipped to the door."

"Special Program Tonight," I read aloud. "Join Ranger Doug Moyer as he talks about the 'Ghosts and Ghouls of the Osage

Hills.' 7 p.m. near Shelter 2 north of the Park Swimming Pool.' Sounds like fun," I said. "Wonder what ghosts he'll tell us about." I stepped inside the cabin; Queenie and Sam followed close behind.

"My guess is he'll focus on the decades of 'white' human history, but you and I know that centuries of Native American history happened here before. Many tribes hunted, traded, and lived in the area."

I laid the flier on the round kitchen table before reaching into the refrigerator to pull out a few of the hamburger patties I'd made this morning. Outside, a motor revved on the road that circled through the cabin area.

"After the past year, don't you have enough fodder in your head for nightmares without adding Osage Hills' ghosts to it?" Sam reached under the sink to get the charcoal lighter fluid and barbecue tongs.

"There's always a bit of real history included in a ghost story. I bet Doug includes Native American folklore and something about the WPA work camp. I want to go." I washed my hands and opened the package of raw chopped sirloin.

"Sure. Maybe you'll come back good and scared. That way you'll hang on to me all night long." He leaned in for a kiss and nuzzled my neck.

Queenie growled low in her throat and trotted into the living room seconds before someone knocked at the cabin's front door. When Sam pulled the door open, Doug Moyer took off his hat.

"Thought I'd let you know the sheriff is still investigating. The deputies have been talking to campers in the tent and RV campgrounds. Park staff is next on the list. And I'm assuming they'll want to talk to your cousin Stephen."

"Stephen? Why?" Sam asked.

"His apiary is near the CCC camp. He's been seen around here the last few days. The sheriff will want to know if he noticed anything unusual."

"I know a couple of his hives were vandalized recently," I added. "He told us it was raccoons."

"Probably. Those critters get into everything. Like bears, they love the sweetness of honey."

Another engine roared as a black SUV pulled into the short driveway and parked behind Sam's truck. John Standingbear hopped out, then moved to the spot near the driveway where he had made the boot cast. He pried it up with a screwdriver, placed it in his vehicle, and walked up to the cabin.

"Hello, again, Jamie. Sam. Doug." He took off his hat and brushed down his black hair. "Stopped back to get the cast of your hiking boots, Jamie. And I need to make one of yours, Sam."

"He was here earlier," I explained. "He needs your boot-prints, Sam. Since we were at the scene of Bridget's death."

"I see." Sam leaned against the doorjamb and pulled off one shoe, then the other.

"Quite a weekend you two are having," John Standingbear said.

"Not exactly what we had expected." Sam handed John his shoes.

"I'll make these casts if you'll get me more water. Jamie?" He handed me the bag of dry plaster of Paris and I went to the sink to fill it with water.

"Here's something new about Bridget," the sheriff said. "Preliminary autopsy revealed bee stings. Most likely the blow to the head killed her, but anaphylaxis—an allergic shock— may have been a factor."

"She was allergic to bees?" Sam asked.

"Must have been. The ME is still tying it all together." He took the bag of plaster of Paris from me. "I'll be right back with your shoes."

Doug glanced at the flier Sam had dropped onto the coffee table.

"You two coming to my ghost program tonight? It's always

a favorite. A mixture of history and mystery, I like to say, with ghouls thrown in for the kids."

"We'll be there," Sam said.

"I was talking to the naturalist, Celeste, this afternoon, and she said that Bridget was a naturalist, too. Do you know if she was trained as a botanist or an herbalist?" I asked.

"I didn't personally have much contact with Bridget, other than seeing her occasionally during a forest patrol. I spend most of the day driving around the campgrounds and the rest in the office doing paperwork before my afternoon patrol. I give my campfire programs on Saturday nights. Routine." Doug put his hat back on.

"Was Celeste the only park employee who had much contact with Bridget?" I asked.

Doug glanced at the driveway, where John Standingbear was making the footprint cast. "Most likely. Celeste is in the park every day, giving walks and talking to people. That's her job. She'd like to get a nature center started up by the tent camp at the old lookout, so she spends time there. You'll have to ask her about Bridget." The ranger waved and headed for the driveway.

The sheriff finished pouring the track and brought Sam's boots back to us.

"Sorry you have to deal with this investigation. Things aren't normally like this around here."

"We know you'll find the answers quickly." Sam shook the sheriff's hand.

"I'll see you both again, soon, under more pleasant circumstances." Standingbear walked to his SUV and slid behind the wheel.

Sam closed the door and slid his arms around me. "Okay, we'll go to the program. I don't think you want to miss out on anything."

I turned in his arms and kissed him.

CHAPTER 10

Sam carried the tray of meat and hamburger fixings out onto the patio. The charcoal glowed red beneath the grate. Queenie lay under the picnic table, her big tongue lolling to one side as she eyed a cricket crawling across the lawn. Sam had lit citronella candles before starting the fire in the grill, and the humid air swirled around us, thick with smoke and insect repellant.

"So your mom wasn't willing to talk about Patrick. You're not surprised, are you?"

"No. I'm not sure how I would feel if I found out she had been in love with someone before Dad. It brings up a lot of questions that I would never ask and she would never answer." I sipped my iced tea. "And some women my age still want to believe our fathers were knights in shining armor who saved our mothers."

"That's okay. But let's talk about reality. How many times have you been in love?" Sam lifted the spatula and held it in midair. "Truthfully. And I'll be just as truthful. Can you remember names?"

I chuckled. "I'd better be able to name names." I took another swig of tea and wished there was something harder in my glass. It wasn't that I wasn't willing to share this information with Sam—I was willing to share my whole soul with him. But some of those 'loves' had not turned out well. Sometimes it was because the man I loved had turned out not to be the person I thought he was. And if I was honest, sometimes it turned out that I wanted something other than love from the man.

"Don't overthink it, Jamie. Want me to go first?" Sam offered.

"No. I can do this." I took another swallow. "First love, Lloyd. Second grade. I was sure he was going to be my forever Prince Charming."

Sam smiled, and lifted his beer as if he was toasting. "To Lloyd," he said.

"Second love, Mike. Fourth grade. Cutest boy ever."

"To Mike," Sam toasted.

"Third love, Jerry. Sixth grade. I thought he was my soulmate for sure."

"To Jerry," Sam toasted. He cleared his throat. "Do I need to get another beer? How many are there?"

I smiled. Puppy loves? Many.

"Seriously," Sam said. "I should have qualified my question. How many times have you been in love since you were, say, sixteen?"

Suddenly, this was serious. I closed my eyes. "Mark, when I was sixteen. I fell out of love and hurt him badly." I knew the pain I had caused. Mark had probably never realized how much it hurt me to have hurt him.

"That's sad, isn't it? I know that feeling, honey." He lifted his beer into the air but didn't toast aloud.

"Rob, when I was nineteen."

"Your first husband."

I nodded. "Who knew when it began that it would end so badly?" I cringed inwardly, remembering exactly how horrific our breakup had been, what life had been like as a single mother with two children and a deadbeat dad, and how, miraculously, Rob had managed to turn his life around and move on.

Sam watched me. He lifted his eyebrows. His warm brown eyes urged me to go on.

"Ben, when I was thirty."

He raised his beer again. "To Ben, and the happiness he gave to my precious wife-to-be."

I sucked in a quick breath and blinked to stem the tears threatening to fall. What a sweet man this was, to toast the other men in my life.

"And you, when I was forty-two." I extended my arms to him.

Sam set his beer on the picnic table and came to me, gathering me up and planting baby kisses on my cheeks.

Under the picnic table, Queenie woofed. A car door slammed.

"Sam? You here?" Stephen called.

Sam pulled away from me. "Company."

"Hey, don't think you are going to escape from completing this same exercise," I teased. "Soon."

"Sam? You got a minute?" Stephen hurried around the corner of the cabin, short of breath.

"Sure. We're cooking burgers. You want one?"

"No time to eat. I need to talk to you."

"Can I get you a beer?"

"I don't want anything to eat or drink." Stephen ran his fingers through his dark hair. He glanced over at me before focusing on Sam. "I need to talk to you. I think I might be in trouble. I did something stupid. Can we go somewhere private to talk?"

"Inside? Honey, can you flip the burgers?"

Stephen rushed into the cabin with Sam on his heels. At the grill, I tended the burgers, an uneasy feeling growing bigger by the second. What was wrong with Stephen?

Eventually, I turned the meat patties and added cheese before I scooped them off the grill with the spatula and onto a platter. A few minutes later, Stephen's jeep started up and drove away. Queenie padded over to the door and whined.

I opened the door and saw Sam at the kitchen table. He looked up, his eyes troubled and dark.

"Honey? What is it?" The uneasy feeling I'd had ever since Stephen's arrival escalated into fear.

Sam scooted his chair away from the table and stood. "Believe me, I'd like nothing better than to tell you what my cousin just told me. But I'm faced with attorney–client privilege. And as far as you are concerned, I can't say a word."

"Can you at least tell me if he's in trouble with the police?"

"Can't say."

"Does this have anything to do with Bridget's death?"

He frowned and stepped away from the table and over to the window. "What do you think?"

"Yes," I replied. Sam looked at me with inscrutable and sad eyes.

CHAPTER 11

Back out on the patio, we prepared our hamburgers in silence. I was full of questions Sam wouldn't answer. What was supposed to be a vacation week of talking about our future had taken a bad turn. Disappointment burned in my mouth.

"Hello! How are you two doing?" a voice called.

I glanced over at cabin six; Bernard and Betty Wood waved. When I returned the wave, they headed in our direction.

"Oh, you're cooking hamburgers. Smells so good!" Betty scurried across the lawn.

"Betty's cholesterol is high. She knows she can't have a burger, and don't you offer her one," Bernard grumbled. The tall man huffed as he tried to keep up. He was inches over six feet, but far from in good shape. What might have once been a six-pack was now a paunch around his middle.

"Oh, there's no problem with enjoying the smell, is there, Bernie?" The woman stopped and closed her eyes, sniffed loudly, and then moaned. "Can't remember the last time Bernie let me have one." She looked up at Sam, round-eyed.

Sam shrugged and looked at me. This wasn't our fight. We had plenty of meat patties.

"Maybe she could have a half of one?" I suggested. "We cooked too many burgers. Why don't you join us?"

"Oh, we couldn't impose. We've got chicken pot pies we were going to pop into the oven, remember, Betty?" Bernard said.

She glared at her husband before smiling at me. "It's kind of you to offer. We'd love to join you. After all, we're going to be neighbors for a few more days, aren't we? At least until Wednesday, when we head back to Wichita." Betty slid onto the picnic table bench and patted the space beside her, glancing up at Bernard for only an instant.

I handed her a paper plate.

Betty prepared her hamburger, spreading the bun with condiments and adding lettuce and tomatoes before cutting the whole thing in two and giving half to Bernard. "I guess you folks got the news. The sheriff and his deputies have been all over the park. Someone found a dead body yesterday in the park."

"How'd you hear about these deaths, Betty?" Sam asked.

"That handsome maintenance man, Chip, told me. But he said there was no need to be afraid. It's not like there's a killer loose in the park or anything." She lifted the burger and took a bite, closed her eyes, and sighed as she chewed. "This tastes like heaven on earth."

"If there's not a killer loose and we're not supposed to be afraid, what did Chip suppose happened?" I asked.

"Chip has the inside scoop. He says the woman was a weirdo. A hermit. She was always doing odd things like climbing trees or singing to the insects in the meadow. Probably a little touched." Betty touched her head with one finger and rolled her eyes. "Killed herself."

"Sounds cut and dried," Sam said.

"Oh, Chip is sure it is. Nothing to worry about. Absolutely nothing." Betty took another bite of her thick hamburger half.

"This Chip fellow seems to know what he's talking about," Bernard said. He inspected his portion of the burger. "Said he's worked here ever since he finished high school. Not much in the way of aspirations for a career, but he seems to know what he's talking about regarding this death."

"No reason to lie to us about it, is there?" Betty added.

"Probably not." I scooped some baked beans out of the pot

in the center of the table and onto my plate. "Did he say any more about the hermit woman? I heard her name was Bridget."

"He did. He told us all about her dead lover. That's why she turned away from society. Sad." Betty took a deep breath and slouched as she chewed.

Doug Moyer had told us the same thing about Bridget after the three of us found her body.

"You'd think this was my first meal in days, wouldn't you?" Betty blurted. "It's not, but it is my first burger in a month. Why is it we want whatever we're not supposed to have? Makes it hard for people to do the right thing."

"Betty, you're rambling," Bernard observed as he wiped mustard off his lip.

"Hm? Oh. Sorry. Tell us all about yourselves. Getting married, aren't you?" Betty asked.

"Yes. This summer," I said.

"Think you might get married here at the park?" Betty asked before taking another bite of her meal.

Sam and I exchanged a glance. So far, we hadn't talked about our future plans.

"It's possible. But this is the first time Jamie's been here," Sam said. "I hope it won't be the last."

"The last? Why? Because of the dead woman? Oh, I wouldn't let that bother me. Cut and dried, closed and tied. Nothing to worry about." Betty smiled, then picked at a bit of lettuce that had caught between her two front teeth.

Sam and I both knew it was not as simple as Betty had heard. Stephen was caught up in it somehow, and he had been worried enough to consult and retain Sam as his attorney of record.

We lingered over our burgers at the picnic table and then after browning the marshmallows over the coals in the grill, we made and savored s'mores. Betty chatted, telling us all about her recent retirement from the personel department at the City of Wichita. Bernard, on the other hand, did not want to retire from the Biology department of Wichita State University, where he taught classes in entomology and invertebrates.

"How anyone could spend thirty years of his life studying creepy crawlies is beyond me," she chided her husband. "So, you are from Pawhuska?' Betty nodded at the two of us as she licked the last bit of melted chocolate from her fingertips.

Sam smiled. "I am, and her family is from the area, but she's lived in New Mexico for most of her life."

"Oh, family ties here? Parents or grandparents?"

"Both, actually," I said. "My mother was Mary Jamison. Her parents lived in Dewey." I thought about mentioning the carving on the old wall and my mother's connection to the camp as a counselor, but before I could, Betty stood and stacked the dirty paper plates.

"Dewey? Is that near here?" she said. "Oh, well. We've taken up too much of your time, haven't we, Bernie?" she said. "We'll leave you two lovebirds alone."

"You two going to the 'ghost and ghouls' talk down at Shelter 2?" Sam asked as she tossed the stack of plates into the trash bag beside the barbecue.

"I know the local history," Bernard said. "Betty, come along."

"Thanks for dinner," Betty called. The pair headed across the swath of lawn toward their cabin.

CHAPTER 12

Two minutes before the program was scheduled to start, Sam and I walked up to the group gathered around the fire ring near Shelter 2.

It had been a quiet journey, both of us eavesdropping on those who walked around us on the road. We had left Queenie in the cabin, hoping that her yips and whines would stop once she realized we were out of earshot.

Sam was firm about what he couldn't tell me about his talk with Stephen, and I was doing my best to accept that fact. If I was going to be an attorney's wife, there were always going to be things he couldn't tell me.

Our marriage would not be like my marriage to Ben. But, I reminded myself, Ben had withheld some important details about his past with me, details I had only found out last fall. He had been full of secrets, even though he wasn't bound by any professional vow to keep them from me.

Our life together would be complicated by the knowledge that when Sam came home from work at the end of the day, his mind might be full of the secrets of his clients. And he could not—would not—share them.

The audience perched around the campfire on split-log benches positioned in concentric half-rings included people of all ages. Most of those who had attended our early morning nature hike were present, plus two dozen more. The Hargis family sat on the front row near the blazing fire. Emma and Jacob fidgeted in their places, ready for the program to start.

Extra pole lights lit the way for people to find seats quickly in the fading daylight. Promptly at 8 p.m., the electric lights flicked off, leaving the crowd in gloom as the sun dropped behind the thick forest. Ranger Doug Moyer picked his way through the benches toward the podium near the blaze.

"Welcome," he began. The ranger made eye contact with each audience member while the logs and branches in the fire cracked and popped. Wisps of smoke billowed into the darkening sky.

"Here at Osage Hills State Park, we have many residents who do not pay taxes or receive bills. We see them only occasionally, but we do see them," the ranger said. "They are the ghosts of the Osage Hills. The area where we now sit is on the Osage Indian Reservation, a reservation created by the federal government for the Osage Nation in 1872 ceding all property here and all mineral rights above and below the surface to members of the tribe."

I shifted on the bench. I knew where this story was headed: back to the bone-chilling story of the Reign of Terror, when over two dozen members of the Osage Nation in Oklahoma either were killed or disappeared.

The ranger described the events of the 1920s and the initial murder of Anna Kyle Brown by unscrupulous white men who desired control of the lucrative mineral rights owned jointly by all members of the 1906 tribal roll of the Osage Indian Nation. As the sky darkened, he told about the other members of Anna's family who were killed or who mysteriously disappeared.

I closed my eyes, dizzy with my own family's story of the Terror as well as with memories of what I had found last year in a tunnel off the root cellar of my family's pioneer homestead.

Sam touched my hand. "You want to leave?" he asked.

"No. He'll move on in a minute." I leaned closer to Sam and felt comforted.

Doug Moyer launched into an account of the explosion that had rocked one home and the dozens of Osage citizens who had disappeared and remained unaccounted for in the years following the incident.

"Their ghosts haunt Osage County to this day. No one knows how many of them walk the earth, seeking retribution for the horrible things done to them by the unscrupulous. Some of them even walk these lands, where they lived long before this property became Osage Hills State Park."

Moyer paused, contemplated the fire, and began again. "Only a few years later, following the stock market crash of 1929, the Great Depression began. Franklin Delano Roosevelt was the President of the United States. Many companies closed. Entire families lost everything; many people who lived in large cities had no food to eat. A new type of criminal activity began. These gangsters, who robbed banks and armored vehicles and stole whatever they could get their hands on to resell, terrorized every state.

"These were real criminals who carried automatic machine guns also known as 'Tommy guns.' Although few people were injured in these robberies and few innocent lives were lost, the FBI was desperate to capture the robbers. Some very well known gangsters took refuge here, in this park, although it wasn't a park yet. These woods provided shelter for the perfect hideout. Old-timers believe the Cookson Hills Gang and its most famous member, Charles Arthur Floyd—also known as 'Pretty Boy' Floyd—kept a hideout in this very park. The gang operated in this region, up into Kansas, and nearly to the Arkansas border for a little over two years.

"People who knew Pretty Boy called him the 'Robin Hood of the Cookson Hills' because he was known to give money and food to those in need. We know his gang hid here, but no one has ever uncovered a hideout or any money taken during a bank robbery." Moyer reached into his shirt pocket and pulled out a coin. "Some of the money they stole may have been silver dollars like this one, a Peace Silver Dollar minted in 1932, now worth about forty bucks." He dropped the coin back into his pocket. "When people see unidentifiable lights in the park on the darkest nights of each month, they know the ghosts of these bandits are roaming the forest, seeking to recover whatever loot they left here and never claimed. Maybe you'll see their lights tonight. Maybe they'll lead you to the money."

In the front row, Jacob whispered in his father's ear. I imagined he was wondering if the coin he'd found this morning in the creek was a Peace Silver Dollar, and perhaps part of the legendary missing gangster loot.

Moyer paused and the audience waited, silent. A few heads turned toward the forest, but there were no pinpricks of light in the trees.

"President Roosevelt created the Works Progress Administration a few years into the Great Depression," Moyer continued, "and within that new department was the Civilian Conservation Corps, a program to put people to work. Young men between the ages of 18 and 24 participated in projects around the country, building bridges, parks, and even picnic shelters. One of the project camps was here in Osage Hills State Park." He nodded toward the nearby shelter and the two massive stone fireplaces on either end of the open-sided structure. "Our incredible stone cabins, walls, bathhouse, bridges, and shelters were all built by these young men."

"We learned all about that this morning," Jacob Hargis shouted.

Doug Moyer smiled. "Then you also know that these men worked hard, keeping little for themselves, sending $25 of their $30-per-month paycheck home for their parents and younger siblings."

Emma Hargis squirmed and whispered something to her father. Moyer was losing his audience.

"But the work was hard. Men became ill and died. They

fought with each other for whatever reason. One was murdered. His ghost is here now."

The little girl sat up straighter and grabbed her father's arm.

"How do I know? Because we're sitting close to where he was killed." Moyer flicked on his flashlight and shone the beam at the stone steps leading from the picnic shelter down to the shores of the creek below. Shadows jumped.

Emma climbed onto her father's lap.

"The story goes that this man, known as Paddy to his friends, was an orphan who'd lost both parents in the influenza epidemic of 1918, when he was only a small child. In 1935, Patrick was among those who first signed up for the CCC. He was 23, almost too old for the program. The story goes that he loved a girl back home in Ohio, where he came from, and that he was saving all his money so that the two of them could get married and he would have a nest egg to buy land to farm, or a business.

"Time passed. He saved his money. Most of the other men sent their money home, but there were also those who spent it on moonshine or gambled it away. One day, the men gathered to receive their payments. Paddy took his pay. When all the money had been distributed, he headed off into the woods. Two men followed him. They planned to find out where Paddy hid his money and come back later to steal it."

I glanced around at the group. The park ranger held them in rapt attention. He stepped around the campfire, picked up a few sticks from a kindling pile, and tossed them on the blaze. The fire roared up, illuminating his face. The pink and orange sunset sky hung above the forest trees behind him.

"Paddy moved through the woods, following a trail he had memorized but never marked. His friends said he was headed for the place where he kept the strongbox with all his money inside."

The ranger stopped, took off his hat, and scratched his head. "They found Paddy's body the next morning, crumpled, lying at the bottom of these steps. And he's still here, searching for his money so he can return to his sweetheart. His money was never found. If you're lucky, *you* might find Patrick Gallagher's strongbox while you're here at Osage Hills."

My look met Sam's. "Patrick Gallagher?" I mouthed.

CHAPTER 13

The surrounding spotlights flashed on. The crowd clapped.

"Thank you all for coming. Enjoy your stay," Moyer said. "Oh, before you go, I have an announcement." Doug waited for the audience to settle down again before he continued. "The park manager has asked me to let you all know that cougar tracks have been seen in this area. Although not common, occasionally, these big cats pass through our rugged valleys."

A few people gasped and an undercurrent of conversation twittered in the group.

"Please, let me speak. Don't be alarmed. Cougars are solitary and nocturnal."

"But I've read about them attacking people," one woman said.

"We've never had an attack here. As a precaution, I suggest you hike or walk the park in pairs after dark or in the early morning. Make lots of noise as you walk. Whistle, laugh, clap your hands. If you do these things, I promise you'll never see one of these cats. Most likely, the animal has moved on anyway."

"Is anyone going to try to catch it? Wouldn't that be the safest thing?" a man asked.

"Our Department of Wildlife Conservation partners in this area will set traps to catch the animal. If you should encounter any cages or traps, please steer clear. Stay on established park trails and roadways." Doug Moyer stepped back from the podium and touched the brim of his hat. "Now, everyone have a good evening, and enjoy your stay."

The audience filed out of the program area and scattered across the lawn. I pulled Sam with me and hurried to Moyer.

"Doug, was your last story based on fact? Was there a Patrick Gallagher in the CCC program?"

"There was," Doug said. "Patrick Gallagher had a wife and baby in Sedan, Kansas. Supposedly he hid money here that was never recovered. But he wasn't murdered. He was injured in an accident during the construction of this very picnic shelter and sent home." The ranger glanced toward the worn, crooked stone steps that led down to the creek. "Makes a good ghost story, doesn't it?"

"Thanks for the info," I said. I grabbed Sam's arm and linked elbows as we walked away from the old shelter and back to the road. "Could the injured worker have been Patrick Gallagher Senior?"

"Your guess is as good as mine. If Patrick 'Paddy' Gallagher was injured, he'd be listed in the official records. Maybe Doug grasped onto the name and used it for his program."

We walked along the road toward the cabin area. Tree frogs croaked, an owl hooted in the distance, and whippoorwills called. The cool, humid almost-summer air was still, enveloping us like a soft cotton blanket.

Our eyes adjusted to the darkness, and the nighttime world appeared. Stars twinkled in the clear sky. We paused in the center of the road and stared up at a million pinpricks of light. Out here, miles away from neighborhoods of homes and well-lit business districts, I could distinguish the colors of stars: they blinked red, blue, and pink.

Sam draped his arm around my shoulders as we strolled down the road.

The tree frog chorus turned up the volume. A family scurried around us, the parents herding the children in front of them and glancing at the dark forest bordering the road. Two of the children clapped their hands, and the other called out, "Here we come, kitty." They moved on, and the sound of their voices faded into the distance.

Sam and I had the road to ourselves as we neared the cabin turnoff.

A dark shape darted across the road in front of us; seconds later, a lonely howl split the air.

"Coyote," Sam said.

I shivered. There were many creatures out and about on such a perfect night as this. Somewhere, the cougar prowled, but it wasn't the cat I was worried about. Humans with ulterior motives could be sneaking through the darkness, too.

CHAPTER 14

Sunday, May 19

Early Sunday morning, I stood in the doorway of the cabin and watched Sam drive away in his little pickup. Queenie whined at my feet. Sam was headed off to talk to Stephen again, this time at his home. Whatever he learned from his cousin would not be shared with me.

Questions had been turning over and over in my mind ever since Stephen's call had roused us both from sleep at dawn. After a short conversation, Sam had rolled out of bed and dressed.

"I need to run over to Stephen's. Not sure when I'll be back."

He was out the cabin door minutes later, and I was abandoned. I had to get a handle on this. Nervously pacing about the little cabin was not going to make me feel any better. I needed a walk.

I snapped Queenie's leash onto her collar and stepped out the back door, locking it behind me. Cabin Trail access lay a few steps away; it paralleled this row of cabins inside the forest before continuing on as the Creek Loop Trail.

Should I walk back to the wall where my mother's name had been carved or to the spot where Bridget's body had been found? I wanted to go back to both places. I remembered the scream. Someone else had been in the woods, and it was her scream we had heard. The sheriff knew it, too.

I stepped onto the gravel path. Queenie tugged on her leash and trotted ahead; she thrust her nose into the undergrowth and snorted. Dead branches and hulking white tree trunks rose from the underbrush.

The forest had the appearance of neglect, but I understood the environmental need to leave the forest alone and let nature take its course. Decay was a necessary arc in the circle of life. Many insects fed on dead trees, along with molds, fungi, and other decomposers. Clutter on a forest floor, beach, or lakeshore wasn't what most people expected to find in nature.

At a fork in the trail, I turned left, aware from the park's trail map that this short branch would lead me to the bluffs overlooking Sand Creek and a view I had not yet experienced. After I had walked only a few steps along the path, murmuring voices caught my attention. Although Queenie was snuffling noisily through the undergrowth, taking in all the rich scents of life, voices and giggles gave away the presence of other people among the trees.

I debated whether to cough or snap a good-sized twig to let the others know I was coming, but at the next slight bend in the trail, I saw them clearly already. A man and a woman leaned against a tree a few yards off the path. The tall man held the slender woman's hands above her head as he pressed against her body, kissing her neck, her cheek, and her ear. His hands roamed across her clothing, and she moaned. The couple's park uniforms made it easy for me to identify them: Ranger Doug Moyer and the seasonal naturalist, Celeste.

I stopped and backed away, eventually returning down the trail the way I had come. The murmuring voices and soft giggles followed me to the fork. This time, I turned left, onto the Creek Loop Trail.

The chirping of birds and hammering of woodpeckers echoed as I strolled along the path. What would have happened if I had announced my presence to Doug and Celeste? Doug would have been upset at being discovered in that position while on duty, as would Celeste.

Queenie snorted and jerked the leash. When she started off at a determined run-walk, I pulled her back. She woofed and strained, wanting to go down a narrow animal trail through the underbrush and into a copse of sumac. She resisted my attempts to pull her back to the hiking trail and charged forward. Broken sumac branches ahead indicated that something larger than a deer had made its way along this trail.

I followed Queenie. She stubbornly fought the leash, eager to be after this new scent. I moved as quickly as I could, avoiding green briar and pushing aside less prickly vines and small tree branches, then ducking as we passed through the sumac grove. I batted away a swarm of gnats. Beyond a small clearing when the trees began again, Queenie pulled me into the thick shadows.

If the dog hadn't stopped abruptly and changed course, we would have passed the structure. Covered with vines and tucked into a trio of blackjack trees with thick, low branches, the shed's weathered wooden plank walls vanished into the natural surroundings. From this angle, the hut appeared small but sturdy. I studied the wall I faced, looking for the door, and finally found it, small and low, near the right corner.

I pushed aside thick strands of ivy to find the latch. When I shoved, the door swung easily open. Inside the dim room, all four walls featured narrow windows installed sideways about two-thirds up the wall. Fabric panels curtained each of them.

Queenie woofed and stuck her nose inside. The rest of her body didn't follow. I stepped inside, down one step to the floor of the hut. At one of the windows, I pulled aside the fabric to let in diffused forest light.

Although only about ten feet square, the room was a fully equipped cabin. A small stove with a pipe chimney sat in one corner and a table and straight chair in another. A narrow bed abutted an adjacent wall. A washstand with a bowl and pitcher stood near the third wall, which was covered with shelving. A padded rocker stood in the center of the room. I coaxed Queenie inside, and she sniffed her way around the room.

Shelves and cabinets covered every available wall space.

Drying herbs and other supplies hung from ceiling hooks and on wire stretched from one wall to another. Woven rag rugs had been scattered on the floor, although wood planks were visible around the stove and in front of the door. The room was neat and cozy, the air cool and clear.

Above me, a lightweight blanket had been hooked to a pulley system on the slanted ceiling; a cord hung down in the center of the room. When I pulled the cord, the blanket folded itself, revealing a skylight. Subdued light flooded the room. The effect was magical. The sunlight caught crystals that hung throughout the room. Vivid splashes of red, green, and blue danced on the walls, furniture, and floor.

The light revealed all of the compact room and the myriad of items it included. One bookshelf held nature guides on Oklahoma insects, mammals, invertebrates, mushrooms, and trees. Another shelf contained books about beekeeping and candle and soap making. I lifted the top of a chest beneath the bookshelf and found beekeeping gear: a netted hat, gloves, and a white jacket similar to the ones Stephen had brought with him Friday. Another large chest next to the stove held pots and pans, baking tins, spatulas, and spoons.

I fingered the neatly folded quilt on the bed and the sweet-smelling cotton sheets that covered a feather mattress. Then I sat down. Queenie plopped down at my feet and rested her head on her front paws.

This had to be Bridget's place. I sensed her love of nature and how content she had been here. I scanned the remaining shelves, each of them a perfect storehouse. Canned food in one section, next to spices. Pyramids of assorted candles and soaps neatly stacked in another. A small pharmacy—bandages, iodine, rubbing alcohol, and aspirin—filled a little cabinet above the washbasin next to a narrow mirror. Bridget's brush, comb, and manicure set rested on the wooden lip of the table holding the washbasin.

I was trespassing. The thought rolled over me, and I immediately hopped off the bed and returned to the low doorway, stooping to look outside before closing the door again.

So this was where Celeste had been caught on Friday, when the sheriff and park personnel had come to investigate after Bridget was found dead. What had she been doing here? Maybe she found the place as comfortable as I did and had only come to visit Bridget, not knowing the hermit had died.

I took one more look around the room. I shouldn't stay. Even though the hut was pristine inside, with no evidence of a struggle or disturbance of any kind, it had to be out of bounds because of the police investigation. Here in the forest, hidden like this, crime scene tape would have advertised the hut's location and defeated the purpose of the tape.

I was drawn to the chest of beekeeping equipment. Bridget was a beekeeper, like Stephen. That was the last avocation someone with a bee venom allergy would take up, I thought. If she was going to be around bees, wouldn't she have worn all the equipment for protection? I lifted out the netted helmet, gloves, and jacket. Beneath were a bee smoker and a slim book—the label on the front cover read *Beekeepers' Journal*.

Inside, written in pencil in small, compact cursive writing, Bridget had detailed her beekeeping activities all the way back to the 1960s. Some entries were only a sentence, others a full paragraph. I flipped through the pages until I reached the last entry of the volume, written about five years ago.

Stephen Knapp has asked for my apiary contract. Del has agreed. This damn allergy has changed everything. Will Knapp allow me a monthly ration of honey and beeswax?

The next entry:

Will sell the hives to Knapp if he wants them.

And then:

No need to tell Knapp anything. He's agreed to let me have wax for soap and candles, and a few quarts of honey as needed. He's using the symbol from the rock as his honey name. Bee Water.

The few remaining pages in the journal were blank.

I reread the entry and my mind worked. Why had Stephen not mentioned that he had taken over Bridget's apiary?

Now he was distressed, and he'd retained Sam as his attorney. It had to have something to do with his relationship with Bridget.

I replaced the journal and the beekeeping equipment in the trunk, then pulled the blanket shade up over the skylight and the drape back over the window. "Come on, Queenie," I said as I stepped outside. The dog hopped up the short step from the interior, then I shut the door and rearranged the ivy to conceal it.

Outside, birds twittered in the trees. A flock of robins flitted past. Queenie moseyed along the deer path again, pulling me past the cabin and down the trail. Only a few yards from the hut, she jerked to a stop, nose to the ground, and nuzzled something beneath a pile of leaves. With her nose, she pushed the leaves aside and uncovered a wad of paper. I stooped and picked it up, then smoothed the page. Even though the page was dirty and some of the letters were smeared, I could make out printed words, written in pencil.

> *Teddy bear, teddy bear, turn around,*
> *Teddy bear, teddy bear, you've been found!*
> *Teddy bear, teddy bear, touch your shoe,*
> *Teddy bear, teddy bear, what will you do?*
> *Teddy bear, teddy bear, go upstairs,*
> *Teddy bear, teddy bear, say your prayers,*
> *Teddy bear, teddy bear, turn out the light.*
> *Teddy bear, teddy bear, say goodnight.*
> *I found you!*

The jump rope rhyme was familiar, but it had been years since I had heard it. The words were different from what I had recited years ago on the playground.

A crow cawed as it flapped overhead, skimming the tops of

the trees. Queenie took off, snuffling through the underbrush along the narrow path. I folded the dirty paper and tucked it into the pocket of my jeans before following the dog. Why was the rhyme here, deep in the forest, and so close to Bridget's cabin?

CHAPTER 15

Fifteen minutes later, Queenie and I emerged from the forest.

White bee boxes dotted the meadow. This must be Stephen's apiary—and Bridget's before that. I counted twelve boxes in the clearing not far from patches of white and yellow wildflowers. One grouping, clustered around a boulder protruding from uneven ground, included a tilted hive. Was that the hive the raccoons had attacked? If so, it still needed reconstruction. I pushed through the knee-high grass toward the boxes, on alert for buzzing bees.

Queenie barked and charged away from me. I let her reach the end of the leash before tugging her back to me. We made our way through the scattered flowers and grass. When I neared the boulders, I noticed a symbol carved in the largest one: two parallel wavy lines, the Native American sign for water. Most likely, the symbol was part of Stephen's Bee Water logo on his honey jars.

A steady line of bees buzzed past me; congregations of bees crawled over the boxes and flew in and out. I steered clear of the hives, circling the area.

If I remembered the park map correctly, I was not far from the old CCC camp. Walking east and slightly north, I should run into it. According to the sketch, the tent camping area and RV park lay immediately to the south.

I followed the meadow to the east until, above the trees, I could see the tall chimney that marked the site of the CCC ruins. The old camp had lost its appeal. Although the brochure I'd picked up at the office had provided the layout of the camp, identifying barracks and common areas, I no longer cared about figuring out what buildings had been where.

I headed for the access road Sam and I had walked, which led to the tent camping area. As I drew near, the wind carried young voices from the tree-hidden ravines. A group of kids were playing hide and seek, pirates, or whatever game kids played when imaginations took over and adults were absent.

On my right, a barbed wire fence bordered the road. Tall clumps of grasses had begun to turn green at the base of last year's dead growth. I picked my way along the road, cautious of the uneven surface. Ahead, a vehicle parked against the fence clued me in to the nearness of the campground.

Park visitors had set up tents and pop-up trailers; their vehicles were parked beneath nearby trees. Campfire smoke hung in the air, and the smell of sizzling bacon and hot dogs made my mouth water. Queenie sniffed the air, and drool dripped from her jowls.

"Easy, girl." I stooped to pet the dog's head. "Sorry to say, nobody's cooking anything for us. Maybe later."

I strolled through the campground. Young children played together on blankets spread in the shade of the old trees, fathers cooked at grills, mothers hung swimsuits on makeshift clotheslines, and teenagers, off by themselves, fiddled with cell phones and iPods.

A short, round rock structure protruded toward the sky at the southeastern end of the tent campground. There was a lookout tower on the map, and although it didn't seem like much of a tower, this had to be it. Steps wound up one side of the squat building to the flat roof. Queenie and I made the climb and stood at the walled edge that overlooked a tree-covered valley and the rolling hills of eastern Osage County.

"Hello again. Great view, isn't it?" a man asked as he joined me on the roof of the lookout. A growl rumbled in Queenie's throat.

"Hush, Queenie. It's okay." I recognized Suzanne and Mike Cooper, the couple who had attended yesterday morning's hike. Both Michael and his wife were fully outfitted again: L.L. Bean from head to toe. Queenie grunted as she dropped down onto the cement roof and stretched out.

"Checking out our end of the park, huh?" Suzanne asked.

"Yes. Lots of fun trails to explore. We visited the CCC camp yesterday but didn't walk through here. I wanted to check out the lookout tower."

"You found it. That elderly couple from our nature hike was up here yesterday afternoon."

"They found someone they knew, I guess. Sounded like they were reminiscing," Mike added.

"Then it must not have been happy memories. The other man sounded sad," Suzanne added.

"How could you tell he was sad?" Mike scoffed.

"A woman can tell." Suzanne glared at her husband. "If you ask me, that man was in mourning. I wondered if he knew that woman who died in the park Friday."

"Was he here at the campground for a while?"

Suzanne shrugged. "When the sun started to set, Mike and I went to the camper to get some marshmallows. When we came back outside, all three of them were gone."

"She doesn't need a full blown history of our night, Suzanne."

The woman smoothed her hair. "We're headed home tomorrow, and I have to say I'm ready to go. Pretty as it is here, there's something about this place that gives me the creeps. Maybe it's the ghost stories, the old construction . . . I don't know." Suzanne tugged at the hem of her vest and brushed at her pants. "You're staying through the week, aren't you?"

"Yes. No changes to our plans."

"Enjoy your time," Suzanne said.

"We will." An image filled my brain. "That coin Jacob found

at the waterfall . . . do you know if he found out anything about its value?"

"Don't think so. He hasn't said any more about it."

The couple crossed the roof to the steps. "You take care, Jamie," Michael called. They disappeared down the stairs.

I wondered who Bernie and Betty Wood had bumped into here at the campground. Knowing Betty, she was wandering around sniffing for a hamburger and an ear willing to listen to her stories. Bernard was her sidekick, but I had the feeling that a little bit of Betty's company went a long way.

I lingered at the lookout a little longer, smelling the scents wafting up from the grills and listening to the children shout as they played. I sought out the source of a repetitive clinking and found several teenage boys pitching horseshoes.

I pulled on Queenie's leash. "Come on, girl. Time to go home." The dog followed me down the steps and out of the campground.

On the main park road, Queenie lagged behind me, her tongue nearly touching the ground as she trudged along. I stopped at the park office and filled the resident dog bowl with water from the hydrant. After a good slurping drink, we set off again down the road.

At the cabin area, the Hargis children were playing kickball in the open field while their mother sat reading on their patio. Bernard and Betty Wood were not outside their cabin.

I unlocked the door, then filled Queenie's food and water bowls and set them outside. I hooked her leash to the doorknob and left the back door open.

Minutes later, as I thought about making sandwiches for lunch, Sam's truck roared up to the cabin. When he stepped inside, I met him at the door and kissed him softly on the lips. Unsmiling and grim, he gave me a quick hug before he walked away from me and into the living room.

I followed him. "Has Stephen been arrested?"

"I went with him to talk to the sheriff. John had requested he come in for questioning. He's not been formally charged with anything." Sam stared through the cabin window at the edge of the forest behind the cabin.

"What can you tell me?"

His brown eyes were sad. "He's a suspect, but I don't know who else is in the suspect pool. They are accumulating evidence." He tucked his long, straight hair behind his ears. "Tell me how your day has gone. Did you get out for a walk?"

"Yes. And unintentionally, I found Bridget's place. A perfect little cabin, hidden in the deep woods. And a trail leads to the meadow where Stephen has his apiary."

His dark eyes narrowed. "Tell me you didn't go inside the cabin."

"Briefly. The door wasn't locked. No police tape. I was only there for a few minutes. But I found something interesting."

"I'm not sure I want to hear this." His face shut down, his eyes went blank, and his lips pressed into a straight line.

I shrugged. "Bridget had a chest with beekeeping equipment in it. There was also a journal. I read the last few entries. The apiary was hers before Stephen got the contract for the Bee Water hives."

Sam tossed me one of his stoic looks. I was reminded of the way he had been last year, when we first met, before we had spent time together and fallen in love.

"Why didn't he tell us that Friday?" I asked. "When we asked about her, he said he hardly knew her. Had caught her taking honey from one of the hives. She may have felt entitled to it if the hives had been hers."

Sam dropped down onto the sofa. "Stephen has over three times as many hives now as Bridget did when she started the apiary."

"I bet he added the hives closer to the wildflower patches, didn't he?" I perched on the edge of the chair adjacent to the sofa.

"I think so. But it was the older hives by that group of boulders that were broken apart last weekend. He says he's had a lot of trouble recently with those hives in particular."

"What kind of trouble?"

"Hives knocked over by the raccoons. Torn apart. Whatever. He wants to relocate them near the other grouping."

"Why can't he do that? Won't the bees come along if he moves the bee box—er, hive?"

Sam shrugged. "I suppose they will. But Bridget was opposed to moving those hives. Stephen said they had been arguing about it for months."

"And that's why the sheriff thinks he might have had something to do with her death?"

Sam stood. "You have violated a crime scene, Jamie. First Stephen, then you. Please tell me you didn't take anything."

"I didn't. I only read the journal. I put everything back as it had been, and I left."

Sam crossed the room. "But you touched things. You left fingerprints."

I recalled the few minutes I'd been inside the hut. "I sat on the bed. I opened the chest and found the journal. I read it. I closed the curtains and left the cabin."

"Great." He shoved his hands into his pockets.

"Oh?" I vaulted up from the chair. "You said Stephen had been there. Is that why he's a person of interest?" I crossed my arms and dropped onto the sofa.

Sam's head jerked and the color drained from his face.

"We're going to have to work through this, Sam. Didn't you have these kinds of discussions about boundaries with Reba?"

Although both of us had been widowed and had talked briefly about our previous relationships, it was the first time I had ever brought her up. I knew he would always love his first wife, and mourn the loss of both her and their newborn baby.

"Reba accused me of doing the same thing, keeping secret

what didn't need to be secret. But I'm concerned about professional ethics, even though the client is a relative."

I jumped up and slid my arms around him. "We can work through this."

Sam pulled back from me. "And we will. I promise. Be patient." His arms closed around me and he pressed his forehead against mine. "Have you thought any more about our wedding? I'm ready."

"I think about it all the time, but we've had a few other things to take care of, you know."

"Can you see it happening here in the park? In October, when the leaves are changing to yellow and orange and the sky is so blue?"

I glanced out the window. Now, in May, the sky was a lighter blue than the one that had hung over us in New Mexico. Still beautiful, but more washed out with the early summer heat. And the clouds stretching overhead had none of the crazy variations of those at home. In New Mexico, it was not unusual to have many different types of clouds filling the same sky, following the air currents that lifted over the rounded hills, into the arroyos, up the old volcanic cones, and onto the pine- and aspen-covered mountains. Puffy clouds; thin, stretched clouds; circular clouds; smears of vapor. There was nothing like it anywhere else.

"October is beautiful in New Mexico, too, with the golden aspen and cottonwood leaves shivering in the breeze."

Sam sighed. "We'll make time tomorrow to talk about this and only this, okay?"

Chapter 16

At the picnic table outside, we ate a light lunch of sliced chicken, fruit salad, and potato chips.

"I need to go back to that wall, Sam," I said as I finished the last bite of fruit salad. "The other names on the wall might jog Mother's memory."

"If she won't talk about the one inscription that mentions her directly, why would she talk about any others?"

I shrugged. "Maybe it will warm her up for a discussion. And give me more to focus on when I go to the genealogy center in Bartlesville tomorrow morning. Can I borrow the truck?"

"Sure. If Stephen needs me, he can come here."

Sam grabbed the park map off the table and traced his finger along one of the trails. "If I remember, that wall was along here somewhere."

"That's where I was headed this morning when Queenie pulled me off that trail and onto the path that led to Bridget's."

"We need to avoid Bridget's house." He rubbed his neck and bent to retie his hiking boots.

"I agree." I slipped a compact camera into my pack. "I'm going to take pictures of the wall. I can send them to Ellen. If Mom won't talk to me about it, maybe she'll spill something to Ellen when she shows her the pictures."

That was assuming my sister would be willing to play an active role in finding out about Mother's life before Dad. After our conversation yesterday, it was doubtful. Unlike me, Ellen had never shown any interest in anything that happened to other members of our family. We had different memories of growing up in the same household. As the youngest sibling, with a brother in between the two of us in age, she had been a bother to me as a child. Time hadn't changed the way I felt; she was still annoying.

I unclipped Queenie's leash from the hook on the back door and attached it to her collar. We stepped out of the cabin and crossed the strip of lawn to the trail.

"It was along here somewhere, wasn't it?" I asked, scanning the lush vegetation on either side of the forest trail. We had found the wall accidentally previously, but I remembered stopping to look at a large white shelf fungus growing on one of the old oak trees right after we'd stepped off the path.

"Here," Sam called.

Queenie woofed and wagged her tail as she trotted off to where Sam wandered among the waist-high vegetation.

Vines and encroaching undergrowth covered most of the old wall, but Sam easily found the carved names. Queenie snuffled in the bushes as I reread the inscription; Sam investigated the old wall.

"There's a large indentation in the earth over here. May have been a building here in the past," Sam said.

I picked my way along the old line of the wall in the opposite direction Sam had taken. It turned a 90-degree corner and headed another way before abruptly ending. Stones of the former wall lay scattered across the ground.

"Do you think the structure was still here when my mother and Patrick Gallagher carved their names into the wall?" I swatted at a mosquito buzzing around my ear.

Sam studied the ground. "Hard to say. Fifty years have passed. There's been nothing to keep the brush and vines from taking over. If the structure was wood, it decomposed or was carried off."

I picked up a stick and moved along the wall toward the inscription, pulling the vines away, searching for other names or dates. I found a few initials but no complete names. "Wonder if Doug Moyer knows what was once here."

"Won't hurt to ask."

A woodpecker drummed into a nearby tree; the sound echoed. I thought about Friday morning, the crashing branch, and the ranger stopping to talk to us. Then the second crash and the scream. Bridget. The crashing tree limb had not killed her.

I kicked over a brick that lay a few feet away from the wall. Two wavy lines had been carved into the top of it. I picked it up and carried it over to Sam. "It's the water symbol. Like on the rock at the apiary. It's the symbol Stephen uses for his honey, 'Bee Water.'"

"If the CCC workers reused existing materials, there could be bricks like this all over the park." Sam tossed the brick down by the wall.

One more unanswered question.

The afternoon air turned sticky, and swarms of gnats and mosquitoes moved in as if we were their afternoon snack. We picked up our water bottles and packs and hit the trail again. Passing through a clearing, I glimpsed clouds building on the western horizon.

I remembered the fierce storm that had rocked my aunt's house in Pawhuska last spring. It had seemed as if the old house would be blown off its foundation during the height of the storm, but afterwards, we'd found only a few shingles in the yard along with plenty of limbs and leaves from the trees.

Hopefully, if there was a storm tonight, it would not turn severe.

I scratched at my neck. Hiking in the woods always made

me itch. Ticks dropped from the trees and chiggers hopped on warm bodies passing through the undergrowth. I imagined members of both insect species working their way up the legs of my jeans looking for tight, warm places.

"I need a shower," I announced. "And Queenie probably needs a bath."

"I don't care if Queenie gets a bath, but I'm willing to help you with your shower." Sam grinned.

We passed the trail junction: one way to the cabin, the other to the cliff overlook at the group camp.

I followed Sam down the trail. When we stepped off the path and onto the lawn, we saw a man peeking into our cabin through the window.

"Can I help you with something?" Sam asked. He strode across the strip of grass to the patio.

"Oh, there you are." The man wiped his palms on his shirt before he extended one hand to Sam. "Chip Erickson. I take care of maintenance. Everything okay in your cabin? Need any light bulbs changed, doorknobs tightened, or anything fixed?"

I recognized Chip as the man who had been using the weed eater yesterday while I'd sat on the patio.

Sam looked to me to answer Chip's question. I shook my head. "Not that we can think of."

Chip glanced from me to Sam. "Thought I'd check. Since you're staying several more nights. Usually, I make a physical check after the third night." His head continued to bob back and forth as he looked at the two of us. "I thought maybe you were inside. Your truck being here and all."

"Everything's fine," Sam said.

"Okay. Have a nice evening. And don't forget about the program up at the group camp tonight. If you like history, you'll be entertained."

"The researcher, Aiden Blunt, is talking about the CCC camp, isn't he?" I asked.

"Yep. He's been doing a lot of onsite research. I've found

him digging around in some of the oddest places in the park. Guess that's part of it, though."

"You know a lot about the camp? Like what was here before it became a park?"

"I know a little. My family is from over to Shidler."

"On the Creek Loop Trail, we found part of an old wall. Was there a structure nearby once?" I asked.

Chip's brow furrowed. "Seems like I heard something about ruins from before the CCC days. An old cabin or shed. Can't 'member where. Might ask the ranger or the park manager, Mr. Snyder."

"Thanks, Chip. I will."

The maintenance man waved goodbye as he rounded the corner of the cabin. Seconds later, gravel crunched on the driveway as his golf cart wheeled out into the cul-de-sac.

Sam unlocked the door. We closed the drapes and pulled off our clothes. Time for a shower and a quick body check for ticks.

Hours later, Sam locked the cabin door behind us as we stepped outside into an oppressive and still evening. The cloud-filled sky was an eerie yellowish green color that deepened minute by minute. The dark clouds were still building to the west and moving slowly closer.

Sam grimaced. "Good thing we've got our rain gear with us. There's going to be a storm."

Warily, I eyed the sky. "Think we should stay here instead?"

He shook his head. "The group camp is the largest, sturdiest building in the park. We're safe there. Hopefully, we'll get a weather update from Blunt when we arrive."

Despite the threat of a storm, I wanted to hear Blunt's program. I intended to ask him about the old wall when the opportunity came.

A dozen people waited in folding chairs inside the main hall of the Osage Hills group camp. Betty and Bernard Wood and Mike and Suzanne Cooper from the RV campground were already seated and waiting. Blunt sat at a table to the side of the room, reviewing his notes. On the wall behind the podium, an aerial photo of the former CCC headquarters was displayed on a screen.

Blunt glanced at his watch and cleared his throat. He moved to the podium.

"I'm Aiden Blunt. Thanks for coming, even with the threatening storm. I assure you we are safe here, safer than you'd be in your tent, RV, or even cabin. We'll hope for the best." He scratched at his chin as he glanced around the room. "I'm here at the park researching for a book I'm writing about the CCC projects in Oklahoma. My research is in progress, but I'll give you a brief update since people expressed interest when they checked in at the park office." He cleared his throat again, picked up a remote, and pointed it at a projector in the aisle between two groups of chairs.

"Here you can see an aerial of the camp in the midst of all the activity here in 1938." He clicked through several more slides before speaking again. Most were photographs I had seen before; they were included in the park's brochure about the CCC camp.

"The CCC program operated nationally from 1933 to 1945. Over two million men and boys participated. This WPA program, part of what many called The New Deal, was intended to 'slow erosion, replant forests, build dams, bridges, buildings and parks, roads and trails, as well as install telephone line,' all while putting people back to work during the Great Depression." Aiden took a long drink of water from a glass on the podium.

"In Oklahoma, one-third of families were on relief. This program allowed people to regain their self-respect, feed their families, and pursue employment. The WPA directed the CCC construction of many different types of buildings besides state parks, including municipal parks, baseball stadiums, schools, post offices, courthouses, and city halls. The camp here at

Osage Hills operated from 1935 to July of 1941 and included over 200 enrollees. Statewide, over 5,000 men worked in 26 camps."

Grainy black-and-white slides of men working flashed on the screen. The men were thin, with sweat glistening on their bare backs and dark, smoldering eyes turned to the photographer. Occasionally, groups of men laughed into the camera, their arms around each other's shoulders.

"Other state parks in Oklahoma constructed by CCC programs representing the humid, wooded areas of the state include Robbers Cave near Wilburton, Spavinaw Hills, and Beaver's Bend near Idabel in the far southeast corner of the state. Roman Nose near Watonga, Boiling Springs near Woodward, and Quartz Mountain near Lone Wolf were representative of the more arid regions. These seven sites in Oklahoma were selected because they were accessible to most of the residents and in areas of historical or geological significance."

I studied the pictures of the men that flashed up on the screen. Many of them reminded me of pictures I had seen at the Osage County Historical Museum in Pawhuska before the fire that had been set to injure or kill me and Vera last year. The blaze had damaged many photographs beyond repair. As I listened, I learned that the government had created a special Native American contingent to the CCC program. Many of my Osage relatives had most likely participated in the program.

"Hush, Bernie." Betty Wood's high-voiced whisper interrupted my thoughts. She and Bernie were seated to my left on the opposite side of the room.

Bernie grumbled something to his wife and stood. "Fraud," Bernie said, scowling. He glared back at Aiden as he stomped from the room; Betty followed him out the door.

I glanced at Sam. "What was that all about?"

He shrugged.

At the podium, Aiden stood open-mouthed, staring after Bernard. "Um. Sorry." He cleared his throat again before shuffling his papers and looking over the audience. "I guess I should open it up to questions."

I was mad at myself for missing whatever had provoked Bernie to leave the auditorium.

"Were there any disciplinary problems at this site with the workers?" a man asked.

"Nothing more than usual when men are thrown together in a closed locality without, um, diversions readily available."

"But what about the man who died? The one whose friends wanted his money? We heard about him at the ghost talk last night," someone said.

"That was a ghost story. In other words, fiction. Didn't happen." Aiden shifted his body and blinked.

"But someone did die here. At the cliffs above the creek," another person said.

Aiden took off his glasses and rubbed the bridge of his nose. "Had nothing to do with the CCC camp. That was years later. Twenty years later."

"What happened?"

"That is not within the parameters of my program."

"Who was it?"

"A young man who worked at the group camp. Apparently, he fell from the bluff outside. Died instantly." Aiden stacked up his papers and stuffed them into a briefcase. "I believe the man's name was Patrick Gallagher."

The audience muttering faded into a buzz in my brain. Patrick Gallagher. And once again my mother had only given up half the story. Why had she not told me that their relationship had ended because he died?

CHAPTER 17

Rain pelted us as we hurried to the cabin. Beneath our hooded slickers, our upper bodies stayed dry as we walked along the road to the cabin cul-de-sac. Trucks and cars passed, throwing spray onto the blacktop, their windshield wipers sweeping rhythmically back and forth. Our heads were dry, but by the time we got back to the cabin, our jeans and shoes were soaked.

Sam unlocked the cabin door and the two of us stepped inside. Queenie greeted us with a 'woof' and danced around, her toenails clicking on the linoleum tile floor. She whined and looked up at us with huge, droopy brown eyes.

"We're back, Queenie. And you're safe. It's raining, that's all," I assured the dog. I slipped off my wet jeans and went to the bedroom to pull on a pair of sweatpants. Sam dug in his suitcase for the weather band radio and set it up in the living room.

Seconds later, a clap of thunder shook the cabin at the same instant lightning flashed outside. I jumped and Queenie tried to climb Sam's legs.

"We barely made it home in time," Sam said. The deluge broke outside. Rain fell in torrents, pounding the roof of the little cabin and pelting the windows.

I glanced around the cabin. "Where is the safest place to be in case of tornado?"

Sam didn't hesitate. "An interior room or hallway. For us, it's the bedroom closet. Every other room has windows."

"Do you think we should get in there?"

"No, honey. This doesn't feel like a tornado storm. Just heavy rain."

"If you say so. You're the expert."

"I've seen a lot of tornados—from a distance. I've been lucky never to have had one actually destroy any family property. We'll be fine." He walked into the living room, dropped down on the sofa, and lifted Queenie into his lap, stroking her back and rubbing her ears. She leaned her head into his hand, sighed, and then closed her eyes. I snuggled up next to them.

He fiddled with the radio, searching for a clearer signal. We listened for a few moments. When the announcer noted that the wall cloud of the storm was passing into west Bartlesville, I sighed. "It's moving east. That means we're out of danger, right?"

"Yes, unless the storm back-builds. We'll keep the radio on, but I think we're in the clear. Just rain for a while longer."

We sat listening to the drumming rain on the roof.

"We've got to find out if that story Blunt told is true," I said. "About Patrick Gallagher."

"Too bad Ranger Doug Moyer wasn't there to confirm it. Or Snyder."

"Shouldn't at least one of the park staff members have attended the program? Seems odd that no one was there, not even Chip."

Sam shrugged. "It was Blunt's program, and he's not a park employee." He yawned and shifted Queenie to my lap before going to the refrigerator, where he pulled out the carton of milk and poured some into a glass. "Need anything, Jamie?"

"No, I'm good." I tucked a crocheted afghan around my legs. "What did Aiden say before Bernie called him a fraud and stomped out? I missed it. Aiden was truly shocked."

"And I'm not sure I heard it correctly. Bernie called him a 'fraud' after mumbling something like 'fifty years hadn't changed who he was.'"

"They know each other?"

"Apparently. And it wasn't a happy reunion."

Sleep eluded me. The pattering of the rain lessened and eventually stopped. I slipped out of bed and padded out to the back patio, taking a kitchen towel to wipe the rain off the picnic bench. I folded the towel and perched on the edge of the picnic bench. The clouds were breaking apart, and as I watched, stars began to spark above me. A bright spot tracking across the sky could have been a satellite or the space station.

Cool, rain-fresh night air whispered against my skin.

A mosquito landed on my arm. I swatted it away. So much for stargazing.

Being at Osage Hills State Park had not been the relaxing getting-to-know-you time I had expected it to be. In reality, it was a getting-to-know-you *process*, and I was seeing what it was going to be like as Sam's wife. There would be ups and downs in our marriage—two previous marriages had taught me that. There would be days I wished I had never taken the marriage vow and days when I would feel so lucky to be Sam's wife.

A fat, furry body waddled out from the trees and over to our trash can. I watched as the raccoon tried to get the lid off. After a few unsuccessful attempts, the animal dropped back to the ground and scurried over to Bernard and Betty's cabin. Seconds later, it disappeared into their trashcan, only to climb immediately out and scramble across the lawn. Mere seconds passed before the raccoon appeared again with two little ones following behind. A family picnic was about to begin.

I stepped back into the cabin and locked the door. In the bedroom, Sam snored softly. I smiled and watched him sleep for a moment before snuggling into bed once again.

I sat up in bed, wide awake. Darkness filled the room. What had awakened me? A noise? I listened to the silence. No. A smell. Smoke. I shook Sam with one hand, kicked off the covers, and rolled out of the bed. "Sam. Smoke!"

He bolted out of bed. With both hands, Sam touched the bedroom door before pulling it open. Smoke rolled across the living room from the kitchen and into the bedroom. "We've got to get out."

I slipped my shaking feet into my flip-flops at the same time I wrapped my robe around my body.

"Queenie!" Sam shouted.

Dog claws scrambled underneath the bed. Sam grabbed my hand and pulled me from the room as I slung my purse over my shoulder and grabbed my phone from the nightstand.

"Queenie, come on," Sam urged.

The dog emerged from the bed and trotted with us from the smoke-filled cabin.

We hurried across the narrow front lawn to the asphalt road and turned to look back at the house. Interior light shone from the windows, but I saw no blaze. What was on fire?

Sam brushed a strand of hair off my face. "Wait here." He dashed across the lawn and back into the cabin.

"Sam! No!" I clutched Queenie's collar to keep the dog from following Sam. My stomach twisted. Shivering, I punched my cell phone's contact directory button and then the phone number for the park office. The telephone system routed me to an operator who answered after-hours calls. "There is a fire in cabin seven. We're outside."

"I'll call for help," the operator said. "We're serviced by a volunteer fire department, you know, but they'll be there as soon as they can. Stay away from the building, ma'am."

Queenie and I huddled by Sam's truck. I watched for signs of Sam in the cabin and prayed for his safe return. Smoke poured from the front door, but no flames appeared. Queenie's distressed yip turned to a bark, and she pointed her nose at the door. Anxiety beat a steady rhythm in my throat and in my head.

"Sam! Come out!" I yelled. The windows of the nearby cabins remained dark. Mercury vapor lights shone onto the asphalt road that circled through the cabins. I folded my arms around myself in the chill night air. In the distance, a dog barked.

"Sam! Where are you?" I called.

Queenie lunged away from me, this time breaking the hold I had on her collar. "Queenie!"

The dog raced across the yard as fast as her short legs could carry her and disappeared into the cabin.

I ran toward the front door. "Sam! Queenie!" Billowing smoke stung my eyes. I coughed and stepped back.

"Jamie? What's going on?" Bernie Wood hollered as he rushed toward me from next door.

"Sam's in there." I coughed in the thick smoke.

Bernie grabbed my arm. "Don't go back in. Sam can handle himself."

Betty huffed up, tying the belt of a thin satin robe as she neared. "Oh, my. What's happened?"

"I don't see any flames. Did you leave something on the stove?" Bernard asked.

"No." I peered through the smoke-filled yard at the doorway. The smoke seemed to be thinning, although it still poured through the doorway. Queenie had stopped barking.

Behind us, a car door slammed. Roy Snyder stepped up. "Mrs. Aldrich? What's happened?" In the distance, a siren shrieked.

"Sam's in there." I knew the panic I was beginning to feel didn't yet show in my face.

"I don't see any flames," Snyder observed. "Maybe Sam already put the fire out."

"Then where is he? He went inside several minutes ago." I chewed at my lip. A terrifying thought struck me. "What if he's been overcome by the smoke? I'm going in."

Snyder grabbed my arm. "Oh, no you don't. They'll have to rescue you, too, after you pass out."

The sound of a second siren split the air as a fire truck finally rumbled up.

Two firefighters dropped off the ladder on the side of the small rural fire truck and dashed toward the cabin, while two more unloaded a thick canvas hose and dragged one end toward the roadside fire hydrant halfway between cabins six and seven.

"They'll have Sam out soon," Snyder assured me. The first two firemen disappeared into the smoke still pouring from the cabin.

"He'll be okay, Jamie. Hang on a minute," Betty Wood said. She patted my arm. I listened for Queenie, expecting to hear her bark. The firefighters called to one another as they pulled the hose across the yard.

A firefighter wearing a thick safety suit walked from the cabin through the thinning smoke and headed for the small group of us standing near the road.

"Nothing's on fire," he reported. "A lot of smoke in the kitchen. We found the source. There's no one in the house. Back door is open."

I glanced around the yard. "But Sam went in. And so did our dog." I started toward the structure.

"No one in there, ma'am. We searched the entire cabin." The fireman took off his fireproof gloves and swiped at his sweaty face.

I blinked. This wasn't possible. Sam couldn't have just disappeared.

"What in the world caused all that smoke?" Betty asked. She stroked my arm.

Bernie shoved his hands into his pockets and shook his head. "I'm guessing that the electrical systems haven't been updated in over thirty years. Simple as that."

"Nothing to do with the electrical system," the firefighter said. "We'll have a more thorough report tomorrow, but I can tell you this: we found a handful of smoke bombs under the sink in the kitchen cabinet. Somebody wanted you out of the cabin." The firefighter trudged toward the fire truck. "Disconnect that hose. No fire here."

"Smoke bombs?" Snyder scoffed.

"I'm going inside." I hurried across the yard; Snyder followed close behind.

As the fireman had said, the cabin was empty. I rushed through the vacant rooms and out the back door to the patio, where I scanned the shadowy tree line for signs of life. The forest loomed dark and silent in the starless night. An owl swooped down from a top branch of the yard's oak tree cluster and disappeared into the forest.

Sam wouldn't just vanish. He had to have left something for me, something to tell me where he'd rushed off to. I examined the small patio area and found nothing.

"Sam? Queenie?" I called. I sank onto the picnic bench. Numbness crept over me, replacing the chill of the humid night.

"You can't stay here tonight," Roy Snyder said behind me in the doorway. "We can accommodate you in another cabin. Number two is empty now."

"I need to find Sam. Maybe he wandered off, injured or confused. This is not like him." I got up and headed for the tree line.

"Ms. Aldrich, stop. We'll have to wait until morning to conduct a search. Can't find much in the dark after such a heavy rain."

"Morning?" I cried. "That's not soon enough. Sam might need help now. He could be hurt. He could have been kidnapped! We can't wait until morning."

Snyder faced me full on, his eyes blazing. "The woods are pitch black. There's no moon tonight. Even with flashlights, it will be difficult to see. And you've forgotten the cougar that could be hunting over the park's acreage. We've set traps, remember?" He frowned. "It's too dangerous. The rain last night will make it easy to find evidence of where Sam and the dog went. Their tracks will be everywhere in the mud. We'll wait until morning. Dawn is only a few hours away."

"Sam? Queenie?" I called. I stared into the dark shadows of the trees, hoping—no, expecting—Sam to walk out at any moment. My heart thudded. Nothing moved at the edge of the forest.

"We'll notify you when the search party has been gathered and is ready to begin. All your clothes probably reek of smoke," Snyder said. "Bag them up and we'll have them washed and cleaned for you."

I couldn't take my eyes off the woods. I scanned back and forth, watching for any sign someone might be standing, watching us from behind the trees.

"There will be a detailed inspection of the kitchen tomorrow by the fire marshal. The state will not rent this cabin again until we'll sure everything is completely safe," Snyder said gruffly.

Tears overran my lower eyelids and rolled down my cheeks. Where was Sam? I wanted to search for him, but all I had, other than the miniscule laser light on my key ring, was the tiny flashlight I kept in my fanny pack. It would be of little use in the dense undergrowth of the forest. As Snyder had reminded me, there was a cougar at large. I swiped the tears from my cheeks with the backs of my hands.

"Thank you," I said, barely above a whisper. I pushed my mind to think about the practical side of leaving this cabin for another. Sam would come back here. If I and all of our belongings were gone, he wouldn't know where I was.

Then, my hope brightened. I could call him, and he could call me. I dashed back into the cabin and to the bedroom. My heart crashed. Sam's cell phone sat on the nightstand beside the bed, still plugged into his charger. I'd taken my phone, used it to call the park office to report the fire. Sam had forgotten to grab his.

I trudged back into the living room, where Snyder waited.

"I need to leave a note in case Sam does come back. And we have food in the refrigerator," I said.

"I'll get Moyer to pack the food up and bring it to you tonight. Leave whatever message you like, in case Mr. Mazie comes back. I'll drive over to the office to get the keys to cabin two and laundry bags for your clothes."

I slipped inside the cabin, bypassing the kitchen, where a firefighter stood at the counter with a clipboard, and walked straight to the bedroom. I pulled our clothes from the dresser and the closet and, after a quick sniff to see whether smoke was evident, laid them on the bed. Then I grabbed our toiletries and personal items, including Sam's phone, and placed them in one of our suitcases.

In the living room, I penned a note on the park notepad from the kitchen counter.

Sam, they've moved me to cabin two because of the smoke. Come ASAP.

It didn't seem like much, but what else could I say in a note that could be read by any curious passerby? I dug in the kitchen drawers for a thumbtack and found one in the back of the silverware drawer. I pushed the tack through the note and then smashed it deep into the wooden frame of the back door. Hopefully, the tack would keep the note in place so that Sam could find it. I hurried to the front yard to wait for Snyder to return.

Bernard and Betty Wood were waiting for me on the lawn.

"You're not leaving the park, are you? What about Sam and the wedding planning?" Betty asked with a pout.

"I'm moving into cabin two for the night." Tears threatened again. I balled my hands into fists and glanced at the side of the cabin. If Sam would only appear. Where was he?

"Oh, you have to be sick with worry about Sam. I don't understand it." She glanced at my tear-stained face and then turned quickly to Bernie. "You know, this makes me think we should leave a day or two early." She absently patted my shoulder.

Snyder's truck rolled through the cul-de-sac and stopped in front of the cabin.

"And not because of that dead woman, either," Betty murmured. "I wonder if it's safe."

"I can assure you it is safe here," Snyder slammed the truck door and hurried to us. "And there's nothing wrong with the wiring in the cabins." The park manager glared at Bernie.

"We'll see you tomorrow, dear." Betty turned her back to Snyder. "And Sam, I hope. I'll miss being neighbors, though." Bernie took Betty's arm and pulled her in the direction of their cabin.

I returned to the cabin bedroom to stuff our clothing into the beige denim sack Snyder had handed me. My legs weakened; I sat on the bed. Where was Sam? And where had Queenie gone? Was she with Sam? My stomach quivered and my hands shook. There would be a logical explanation. I wanted to believe that with all my heart.

Back outside, I handed the bag of smoky clothes to Roy Snyder.

"You'll let me know first thing about the search?" I asked.

Snyder nodded. "It will be early. Crack of dawn. I'll get on the phone right now and get people lined up to help, including the sheriff and his deputies."

"Thank you." I climbed into the front seat of Sam's Ford Ranger. One last glance at the cabin showed lights blazing from each window and emergency lighting still focused on the structure. I scanned the yard and the line of trees, but there was no movement.

I didn't want to leave, but why stay? There was no sign of Sam or Queenie.

A few minutes later, I stepped into cabin two. The floor plan was identical to our other cabin; the only thing missing was Sam. Every part of me ached with the agony of not knowing where he had gone or why.

I unpacked our toiletries and placed them in the bathroom

before throwing myself on the bed fully clothed. Every light in the cabin was on. I placed my phone on the nightstand next to the bed.

Sam would be back soon. I had to believe that.

CHAPTER 18

Monday, May 20

After a few fitful hours of catnapping, I rolled off the bed and trudged into the living room to stare out of the cabin's picture window, watching the sky lighten from black to gray. I studied the woods and my heart ached. Where was Sam?

And as if that wasn't bad enough, I was worried sick about Queenie. Was she with him? Were both of them hurt, lying in the forest, unable to get back to the cabin? Even worse, what if she had encountered the cougar? Her thick basset hound frame and short legs would be no match for the mountain lion.

Someone knocked at the door. I rushed to pull it open, hoping to see Sam smiling in at me. Instead, Sheriff John Standingbear loomed in the doorway.

He squinted into the dark cabin, holding his hat in front of him with both hands, as I unlatched the chain and opened the door. "Have you heard from Sam?" he asked gently.

I shook my head and stepped back, motioning him to come inside.

"It must have been something very important for him to leave without telling you anything."

"What could be that important?" Tears sprang to my eyes. "This isn't like Sam. I'm worried."

Standingbear's forehead wrinkled and worry clouded his eyes. "Before we jump to conclusions, we'll search. Around the cabin and in the forest. There will be signs of where he went."

"When?"

"Volunteers are gathering at the park office now. They'll head over to cabin seven shortly. Do you want to go with me?"

"Let me grab my pack," I said, turning to the bedroom.

"Can you bring an article of Sam's clothing? Something not yet washed? I've requested a K-9 unit, and they'll need a scent sample."

"It all went into the clothes bags I gave to Mr. Snyder. To be washed because of the smoke."

"Is there anything else? A pillowcase or towel? A hairbrush?"

"At cabin seven there is, if they haven't pulled the linens off the bed yet or washed the towels. And I have his hairbrush."

He nodded. "Good. We'll check at the cabin. I'll wait for you in the truck."

Taking time only to wash my face and brush my teeth, I tugged on my boots, grabbed my fanny pack, and darted from the cabin. I climbed into the cab of the sheriff's SUV.

"There's insect repellant in the side pocket there," Standingbear said. "If you haven't put any on yet, I suggest it."

I found the repellant towelette and rubbed the saturated pad liberally on my arms, neck, and face. Insects favored me over anyone else in a group, with chiggers, mosquitoes, and even ticks finding their way into my clothes if I didn't take precautions. The truck's cab filled with the citrus-sweet scent of the repellant.

The sheriff swung the truck around the cul-de-sac and into the driveway of cabin seven. A dozen people already waited in the front yard. Birds twittered in the surrounding oaks and elms. The members of the search party gathered around as we stepped out of the truck and onto the lawn.

"You've all been briefed on the situation," the sheriff began. "Sam Mazie is a local attorney. He disappeared in last night's smoke incident at this cabin. A K-9 unit from Bartlesville is on the way. When they arrive, we'll head out."

Standingbear steered me toward the cabin. "Would you check on the bed linens? I'll wait out here." He unlocked the front door.

I stepped inside, where the scent of smoke lingered. The linens were still on the bed. I jerked the case off Sam's pillow.

Outside, I handed the pillowcase to the sheriff. "I hope this will help."

"Should be enough. Here comes the K-9 unit now." A black Chevy Blazer rolled up with *K-9 Search* printed on the doors. A man and a woman jumped from the vehicle and hurried around to the now-open back hatch. Seconds later, a small German shepherd leaped out of the back of the vehicle, wearing a thick black harness bearing a K-9 unit insignia and hooked to a long leash. The animal flicked its ears, then trotted at its handler's side as the group made its way across the lawn to us.

"Sheriff Standingbear?"

After the sheriff nodded, the woman continued, "SAR volunteers Marx and Jeters reporting for duty with Samson." She reached for the pillowcase in Sheriff Standingbear's grasp. "I'm Darla Jeters. Is that a scent sample?"

John handed the folded polyester material to her. She squatted beside the dog, allowing him to sniff the pillowcase and nose it. The dog looked at her and whined.

"Before we start the search, you need to know a cougar has been sighted in the area. Some traps have been set. Is that a problem?" the sheriff asked.

The second volunteer stepped up. "I'm Eric Marx. I'm assuming your traps are set along known animal trails? Ravines and so forth? I doubt our search will take us there, but if it does, we'll be on the lookout."

"We're ready," Darla Jeters said.

Samson tugged at his leash as Jeters led him into the cabin. The sheriff and I followed, while the rest of the group circled around to the back yard, where the trail led into the forest. The shepherd trotted from room to room, lingered in the bedroom, and then dashed to bark at the back door. Standingbear unlocked it and the dog charged through, barking, pulling Jeters along. She jogged behind him across the lawn and onto the trail.

The search team spread out, trekking through the thick undergrowth of sumac, buckbrush, and vines, watching for any clue Sam had passed that way. The searchers on each end of the line of volunteers repeatedly called his name. Sheriff Standingbear and I picked our way down the trail, watching and listening for any indication one of the searchers had found something.

The search party moved slowly through the woods. I could hear Samson in the front of the group, barking, on the trail to finding Sam.

Seeds of worry began to sprout in my head and in my heart. If we did find Sam, would he be injured? Would he be dead? I began to hope we didn't find him. That way, there was still a chance he might walk up to the cabin later today with some crazy story about what had happened to him.

We trudged through the underbrush.

"Sam? Sam Mazie, are you here?" the searcher on the far end of the line called.

"Sam Mazie? Can you hear me?" another searcher shouted from the opposite direction.

The line progressed forward slowly. I watched the ground like the other searchers did, looking for evidence Sam had passed this way, either voluntarily or involuntarily. My eyes watered from staring at the confusion of twigs and rotting and fresh leaves littering the forest floor. The scent of earth and decay filled my head, laced with wisps of citrus-scented insect repellant.

CHAPTER 19

My brain suddenly registered silence. Samson had stopped barking. The volunteers were clustered on the trail. The sheriff and I shoved through a grove of sumac bushes to join the searchers.

"We've found nothing, Sheriff. No tracks, no sign," one of the deputies said. "His scent is here. Looks like the trail doubles back. At least that's what Samson is smelling."

I glanced around the area and recognized the stump of a dead tree and a long scar on another caused by a lightning strike. The vine-covered wall was several yards away from where we were standing. "We were on this trail yesterday."

Darla Jeters spoke up from where she stood a few feet back up the trail. "Samson is picking up those scent signals. Even though it rained last night, the smells are still there. Possibly even accentuated by the rain. Did you return to the cabin from here?"

"Yes. Followed the trail."

"I don't believe Mr. Mazie came this way last night," she said.

"We should go back and search the lawn and the cabin area more thoroughly," Snyder suggested.

I looked at him, surprised that both he and Ranger Doug Moyer, who stood beside him, had joined the search. Neither of the men had been at the cabin when the search began.

"Last night, we swept the immediate area around the cabin

and throughout the cul-de-sac," Snyder said. "I suggest we return there and see if Samson can find a trail."

Downhearted, I watched the searchers spread out again and return through the forest. The search and rescue team trotted ahead along the trail, Samson still with his nose to the ground and low tail sweeping from side to side.

Where was Sam? Instead of feeling relief that we hadn't found an injured Sam, my head filled with dread. What if we never found him? What if he'd vanished, like so many of the women I had learned about last fall in Las Vegas, New Mexico, when I'd been searching for my stepdaughter? What if I never heard another word from him? What if I never knew what happened to him?

The thought was unbearable. My hands shook.

I had to believe we would find Sam. He was alive, and so was Queenie. I would search until I found both of them.

Back at the cabin area, the searchers spread out again. Samson had another nose full of the pillowcase's scent, and he pulled Darla across the back lawn, barking. Sheriff John Standingbear and I brought up the rear, staying a good twenty yards behind the SAR team as the others fanned out across the green expanse. Samson reached the asphalt road and stopped. He whined and whirled in a circle. After a few seconds, he sat and looked up at Jeters.

"That's it," she said when the sheriff and I jogged up. "The trail's gone dead. My guess is that Mr. Mazie got into a vehicle. I don't think we're going to find him in the park."

My body felt oddly heavy. Not in the park? Where had he gone?

John Standingbear sighed. "I'm sorry. I promise we'll keep looking. I'll issue a COS with his description. Maybe someone saw something either in the park or in the surrounding county. Do you have a recent picture of Sam?"

"A COS? What do you mean?"

"It's police jargon. COS stands for 'check to your own satisfaction.' Sam isn't a fugitive, and we haven't any proof he didn't voluntarily disappear. A COS means everyone will be on the lookout, and if they find him, they'll confirm he is not injured or under duress."

I hadn't thought it possible to feel any more down, but I did. Was it possible Sam *had* voluntarily disappeared?

"Is there a picture? Perhaps on a camera, or your cell phone?"

"Let me think." I searched my brain, trying to recall if I had a picture of Sam with me. I had photos at my house in Las Vegas, New Mexico. I had photos in Pawhuska at Elizabeth's house, and his mother certainly had plenty of pictures at her rural home north of town. "I'm sorry. I don't have one here." I swiped at my forehead where I'd felt the feathery touch of an insect.

"We can probably pull something up off the internet. From the Osage tribe, the courthouse, the bar association. We'll find a picture to use, Jamie."

I nodded and scanned the faces of the searchers who'd traipsed through the forest looking for Sam. "Thank you all for helping with the search. I appreciate it, and Sam's family will, too."

A few people muttered, "You're welcome."

Another said, "Sorry we didn't find anything."

"We're going to keep searching, Ms. Aldrich," Roy Snyder said from behind me. "Ranger Moyer will be on patrol in his truck, watching out for anything the least bit suspicious, and I'll be on patrol today and tomorrow, too. If Mr. Mazie is still in the park, we'll find him."

"Thank you," I said. There was nothing else to say.

I wanted to be alone.

I headed toward my new cabin. After a few steps, I sensed someone following. Sheriff Standingbear nodded when our eyes met; we walked together to the cabin.

CHAPTER 20

"Jamie, you have my promise. We will find Sam." John Standingbear laid his hand on my arm as we reached the cabin's front door.

"You don't know that. I'm afraid." My hand shook as I pulled the key from my pocket and inserted it into the door.

He sighed. "You're exhausted. Try to get a little rest. I'll call this afternoon if there's any news." He stepped off the porch, then turned back to me. "We'll find him."

Inside the cabin, with the door closed and locked, my legs folded beneath me. I sat in a heap and sobbed.

Eventually, I got up and trudged into the bathroom, stripped off my clothes, and took a shower. John Standingbear had told me to rest, but I couldn't think about lying down and trying to sleep. I needed to find something else to occupy my time; otherwise, my fears about Sam and his safety would eat away at me.

In the little kitchen, I dug out the coffeemaker and filled the carafe with water. I jumped when someone knocked on the front door. If Queenie had been here, she would have alerted me. I said a quick prayer for her safety. *Please let her find her way back to me.*

I left the chain lock in place and peeked through the crack.

Celeste smiled in at me. "I heard about the smoke scare last night and the search this morning. I'm sorry I couldn't have been here to help."

I undid the chain. "Come in. I was making coffee. Do you want some?"

Her gaze swept the room. "Sure." She rubbed her palms on the khaki shorts she was wearing. "Still no word from Sam? Anything turn up during the search?"

"No." I returned to the kitchen. "I don't get it. This is so unlike him." I placed a coffee packet in the coffeemaker, closed the lid, and pressed *On*.

"Doug said he was going to drive the park service roads," Celeste called from the living room. "He'll watch for anything unusual. If Sam is in the park, he'll find him."

"But what if he isn't in the park?" I watched the dark brew trickle down into the carafe. Celeste didn't respond. I closed my eyes, leaned against the kitchen table, and dropped into a chair.

Celeste appeared in the doorway. "I overheard something . . ." She swallowed. "I mean, you need to know that after this morning's search, they don't think he's in the park. The sheriff will follow up on the possibilities." She chewed her lip. "There was no evidence of foul play. They don't think anything happened to him or anything like that."

I rubbed my forehead. "I want to know where he went."

Thoughts rolled through my mind. Disappearing without any word to me was so unlike the Sam I had come to know and love. I refocused on the incident. The sheriff was following up on 'possibilities.' One big possibility sprang into my mind. *Stephen.*

Celeste pulled the other kitchen chair out from under the table and sat. "Tell me about the smoke bombs. I'm glad it wasn't a real fire. Who do you think put those in the cabin?"

The coffeemaker huffed. I got up, poured a cup for me, and filled another for Celeste.

"That's a good question. Maybe someone wanted us out of the cabin." I sat at the table again.

"Could be. But Sam went back in. Who would expect him

to behave that way? Maybe the purpose of the smoke was to separate you, not just get you both out of the cabin."

I considered her suggestion. Once again, the first person who sprang to mind was Stephen.

"What are you going to do?" she asked, taking a tentative sip of coffee and then setting the steaming cup back on the table.

"For starters, I'm not going home. I'll stay the week in the park as Sam and I planned. I'd intended to research some area history today. I guess I could go ahead and do that. Anything would be better than sitting here, worrying." I rubbed my cold fingers against the hot mug.

Celeste nodded. "Best to keep busy. Can I help in any way?"

I forced my mind to consider the other things I was going to investigate. Bridget. And Patrick Gallagher. "Has anyone learned any more about Bridget's death? I'm still curious about her. No one seems very willing to talk about her. Why was she living out here?"

"She chose to be here. I'll never understand why." Celeste glanced out the rear window before she turned back to me. "I cared about her, you know. I think I was her best friend."

"You've worked here before this summer, haven't you?"

"Yes, but I first met her when I came for camp as a teenager. She led some nature activities. Actually, she's the reason I fell in love with nature. This is my fifth summer out here."

"And what do you do when you aren't being a seasonal naturalist?" I was fairly certain I already knew the answer.

"I'm a fourth-grade teacher. In Bartlesville."

"Makes sense. You love ecology and botany, though, or you wouldn't be here during your summers talking to people about the Cross Timbers region."

"I do love it. Even the heat and the bugs. But it won't be the same ever again. I'm going to miss Bridget. She was my mentor. She taught me most everything I know about the woods, and you can't learn many of those things in school."

She ran her hands through her short blond hair and scooted to the edge of her chair.

I thought about my great aunt. She'd been my mentor in much the same way when I was growing up. "Stephen told us Bridget was a beekeeper, that she managed the hives before he took over the apiary."

Truth be known, Stephen hadn't exactly been forthcoming about their relationship. Did Celeste or any of the park staff know the police had talked with Stephen about Bridget after her death, and that he had retained Sam as his attorney?

"She was a wonderful beekeeper. The bees loved her," Celeste said.

"Is that possible? For an insect to 'love' a person?"

"Oh, yes. Bees are sort of like dogs in that way. They know if you're frightened of them. They smell fear. But Bridget said it was always good to take precautions, to wear the netted hat and gloves especially. She wasn't much for wearing her jacket, though, except for when she was harvesting honey."

"But Bridget hadn't worked with the bees since Stephen took over, had she?"

"Oh, sure. She helped him each week, checking the hives when he couldn't make it out for a few days," Celeste continued. "Recently, she removed the mouse guards when Stephen was too busy to do it. Sounds funny, doesn't it? But the guards keep the mice out of the hive during the cold months. They can do a lot of damage."

"And Stephen paid Bridget in honey and beeswax."

Celeste nodded. "He let her take whatever she wanted, but Bridget didn't want much. She made candles for her own use—lots of candles—lotions, and even soap. After she harvested the beeswax, she'd make candles for gifts and to sell. When I couldn't take her, Doug would drive her over to the Keepsake Candle Factory to use their equipment."

"Doug? The ranger? I remember him saying he didn't have much contact with Bridget."

"Oh, he liked Bridget. But he didn't seek her out. She would let him know when she needed a ride to town. The only person she ever had trouble with was Snyder." Celeste's face hardened.

"Trouble with Snyder? Did he want her to leave the park?"

Celeste pushed her chair away from the table and glanced at her watch. "He said she was a liability. If anything happened to her while she was on the property, she might sue the Park Department. And if she stole park property or some visitor's belongings, legally, Snyder would be held responsible since he allowed her to live here."

"Did she ever steal anything?"

"Of course not. Why would she? She didn't use much, and she had everything she needed."

"So, did she ever tell you why she was living here?" I pressed. "I've heard the stories about her dead lover."

Celeste raked her fingers through her hair. "Those stories must be true. A young man—a teenager—died at the overlook. But I don't think she was here because she 'wanted' to be near him, like the stories say. Otherwise, wouldn't she have hung out at the overlook? She never went there." Her cheeks flushed.

I stared at her. My brain clicked. Was she talking about Patrick Gallagher? My mother's Patrick Gallagher?

Celeste took a long sip of coffee. "I think she was living out here because she was hiding."

Coffee sloshed from my mug onto the table. "Hiding from what?"

"Who. This is my theory, anyway. I think she was hiding from whoever threw that teenager off the overlook. I think she saw it happen."

A chill crept up my back. No one had ever mentioned murder in connection with the younger Patrick's death. What was the truth? The silly jump rope rhyme I'd found popped into my mind. The final words, changed from the original rhyme, were 'I found you!'

Who had found her? Had Bridget's death been caused by the person who wrote the nursery rhyme note?

CHAPTER 21

Celeste glanced at her watch again. "I'd better get back to work. I never intended to stay this long." She smiled. "You're easy to talk to, and I guess I needed to talk to someone about Bridget. I still can't believe she's gone."

"Have you talked with Doug about her?"

She shrugged. "Doug didn't like her as much as I did." She blushed again. "And we don't talk about personal things."

"Celeste, I have to tell you something. I saw you and Doug in the forest yesterday morning. And you didn't seem to be just 'friends.'"

Her face blanched. "You . . . saw us?" She set her empty mug on the table and stood.

"I did. I was hiking. I immediately turned around and went the other way, so I didn't see much, but it was enough to know the two of you are romantically involved."

"Oh," she said, looking out the window. "I never intended to . . ."

"Whatever is happening between you and Doug is none of my business. I don't know much about either of you. But I know how good it feels to be in love . . . most of the time."

One of those times it didn't feel so good was now, when my heart ached. I was filled with confusion, and with fear for Sam.

"So will you keep my secret? I don't think Snyder would be too happy if he knew." She frowned and chewed at the end of one fingernail.

"How long have you and Doug been dating?"

Her eyes lit up. "We flirted a little last year, but he was still married. He called me over Christmas break, and we started dating last spring after his divorce was finalized." She grinned shyly.

"Have you ever been married?" I asked.

"No. The right guy hasn't come along. I'm twenty-eight. And I think it's finally happened."

"Have fun with Doug. He seems like a nice man." I didn't tell her that he also seemed like a man who didn't always say what he thought. Could be he didn't hold back with her.

Her eyes twinkled. "Oh, he is. We have a lot in common, with our love of nature and our interest in history. He's always doing research on the park. He draws from that for his 'ghost' talk. And he's been learning a lot about the Depression days and the bank robbers and gangs."

I remembered the coin he had shared with the audience during his ghost talk and the 'ghost' with the same name as the boy on the wall. "Has he ever talked to you about that teenager? Not the CCC worker whose story he fictionalized to create a ghost, but the younger man who fell from the cliff at the group camp and died? I think his name was Patrick Gallagher, too."

"It was?" She edged toward the door. "Doug hasn't talked to me about it. Crimes or deaths that happened in or around the park are part of the history training we all have to take before working here. You never know when some 'fan' of gruesome stories will show up, or a local who wants to talk about the old days."

"Have you had any weird 'fans' in your summers here?"

She tilted her head. "I haven't. I think Doug has, and recently, too. You'll have to ask him. Now, I have to go. I have my weekly conference call with the Oklahoma City office in ten minutes." Celeste pulled the cabin door open. "I'm thinking good thoughts about Sam, Jamie. He'll show up. Probably today. I could see in his face how much he loves you."

I followed her to the door. "I hope he'll come back today. I still can't believe he's missing."

"I'll see you again soon. I do a nature walk on Wednesday mornings. Join me if you're still here. We take the lake trail and end up at the old lookout at the tent camping area. Could be an entirely different group of visitors by then."

"We'll see what happens. Thanks for coming by." I shut the door behind her and turned away, closing my eyes.

Wednesday was two days away. Surely Sam would be back long before Wednesday, unharmed, with a logical explanation for his absence. The alternative was unthinkable.

I pulled out my cell phone. Although it was an hour earlier in Rio Rancho, New Mexico, I knew Mother was already up. She had told me numerous times that the older a woman gets, the less she sleeps.

I had so many questions about Patrick Gallagher and her relationship with him, as well as about Bridget. There had to be more she could tell me.

The phone rang three times before she answered.

"Mother, do you have time to talk?"

"Oh, Jamie. I hope this isn't about my name carved into that wall again. I'd rather you forgot about that."

"I can't forget about it, Mother." A nugget of a headache began behind my forehead. Right now, finding out about Patrick Gallagher was only a diversion. I had to pursue it or else lose my mind waiting for news of Sam.

"It was an unpleasant part of my life. Why can't you leave it alone?"

"I've heard more of the story since we last talked. Your relationship didn't just end. He died—he fell from the overlook."

The ensuing silence on the other end of the line told me the story was true. The Patrick whose name was on the wall with my mother's and the boy who died at the overlook were one and the same.

"Oh, Jamie," she finally groaned.

"Did you see Patrick Gallagher fall?"

"Oh, Jamie Lynn. No, no, no, no, no," she groaned. "Leave this alone!"

"Mother, talk to me. Please. I told you about the old woman, Bridget, who died last Friday. I think you knew her. Was she around that same summer?"

"Jamie, please."

"I've just learned that Bridget may have been living out here because she was hiding. And now she's dead. Did someone kill her because of something that happened all those years ago, during that summer when Patrick Gallagher fell? Mother, is it possible someone murdered Bridget?"

"I don't know. I really don't know." Her voice shook.

I waited, hoping my silence would pressure her into talking to me. Either that or she would hang up.

She sniffed and let out a long breath. "Bridget was my best friend. Long before camp."

I gasped. I had not expected this, only that the two of them had been acquaintances.

"We went to camp that summer in high school and we met Patrick. She had a crush on him. I didn't want him to . . . *like* me. Because of the way she felt about him. But he did. And I was silly about it, flattered at the attention, especially at first."

"Tell me what happened."

"Oh, Jamie. Nothing happened between us. Bridget was hurt, but she knew I hadn't tried to get him to like me. I just didn't discourage him. He was handsome, careful about his appearance." She cleared her throat. "He laughed at my jokes as well as at Bridget's. We were more of a threesome than a couple."

"So you dated, and he carved your name in that wall."

"Is there anything left of that old shack?"

So Sam's suspicion was right: a building had stood in the yard bordered by the wall.

"No, there's no evidence of a building, and the wall has fallen down completely in some places. People have carried away the bricks."

"But you found the carving of our names."

"Yes. And I'd really like to hear the story of your romance. Were you two serious?"

"Jamie Lynn, I was too young to be serious. My best friend was in love with him."

"What happened at the overlook the night he died?" I blurted. I couldn't shake the feeling that the events of that night and Bridget's death had something to do with Sam's disappearance.

"That story has become part of the history of the place, hasn't it? They probably say his ghost haunts that patio, don't they?"

"Actually, it's not *his* ghost who is part of the ghost stories. It's another man named Patrick Gallagher, one of the CCC workers."

"You mean Patrick's father. But he didn't die there. How could he be a ghost?"

"I think the ranger who wrote the program combined the two stories. He told about the ghost of Patrick Gallagher, a man in the CCC program who had been murdered for his money stash. He didn't explain there were two Patrick Gallaghers. But back to that night, Mother. What happened?

"Money stash?" she said in a low voice.

"Yes. According to the 'ghost' story, he'd been keeping his money rather than sending it home. He was killed when he wouldn't turn it over to a gang of thugs, or so the story goes."

"Patrick's father went home when the CCC camp disbanded. He was still alive when his son died. It was a tragedy."

"How did it happen?" If I asked enough times, she might actually tell me.

She sighed and then began. "A whole group of us were outside the dining hall. The boys were being silly. Daring one another to run along the edge of the cliff overlook." She paused, and I imagined her eyes closing as she remembered. "The camp director caught us and made us all go to our cabins. Bridget and I told Patrick goodnight and went off to our cabin, which was down the slope from the patio at the dining hall."

She pulled in a deep breath, and when she spoke again, her voice shook. "The next morning, someone found Patrick in Sand Creek, below the overlook. Dead." Her voice dropped. "We couldn't believe it."

"What happened after that?"

"We all went home. Bridget and I never talked about Patrick again. We lost touch after I married your dad." She cleared her throat. "I haven't thought of her in years. I had no idea she was living at the park. A recluse . . ." My mother's voice broke. She was sobbing again.

"What was Bridget like?" I couldn't seem to get past wondering why she had retreated to live alone in the forest. Celeste's suggestion that she had been hiding nagged at me.

Mother sniffed and breathed out a long breath before she spoke again. "She wasn't reclusive when I knew her." She swallowed. "Bridget was the life of the party. That made it even harder to understand why Patrick didn't fall in love with her. It wasn't for lack of trying on her part."

"She flirted with him?"

"He wasn't interested. And I don't think I'd have been able to prevent his interest in me, even if I had wanted to."

"You encouraged him?"

"I didn't *dis*courage him. He was handsome. Most of the other girl counselors and half of the campers had crushes on him."

Mother's voice had calmed, and I heard some good-natured humor in her tone. I had to keep her talking before her emotions got the best of her again.

"You said she was the life of the party. Was she a good student, too?"

"In certain subjects. She liked science and math, and there were few girls who excelled at those subjects back in the fifties. If a girl did excel, she didn't let on. Girls were not expected to speak up in class or to act knowledgeable about anything. I knew she was smart because I had so many classes with her. She helped me the most in math."

"Did she go to college?"

"Back then, women rarely went to college. Society expected young women to marry after high school. If we went to work, we were teachers. Some girls went to business college and became secretaries."

"What did Bridget do after high school, when you married Dad?"

"The last I knew, she had a job at Woolworths in Bartlesville. She talked about becoming a teacher, and as far as I knew, she was saving money to go to Central State Teacher's College in Edmond."

"Did she?"

"I don't know. I had a husband, and soon the three of you came along. For women, life in the fifties and sixties was about family. As mothers, we gave up selfish dreams."

"Not everyone did, Mother. Some people pursued their dreams."

"No one I knew did."

"But you got married. You found love."

She laughed. "Yes. Back then, just like these days, people dreamed about love. All the top movies were about love. Pop songs on the radio, and even on TV, were about love. Doris Day was every guy's dream girl. Most of us wanted to be like her."

I thought about the song I'd heard Aiden whistling. "Secret Love" had been a Doris Day song. And Aiden was of my mother's generation. "Bridget must have been lonely if all of her friends got married so quickly."

"She probably was. I don't know."

"The park naturalist here said Bridget knew everything there was to know about the Cross Timbers and the prairie, like Aunt Elizabeth. She made her own soap and candles, collected herbs, and kept bees."

"I'm not surprised."

"How does someone go from being the life of the party to

being a recluse? Do you think she could have been hiding from someone?"

"No," she said, a little too firmly.

I remembered the crumpled note I had picked up from the forest floor near Bridget's hut. "Mom, does that old jump rope rhyme, 'Teddy Bear, Teddy Bear, turn around,' mean anything specific to you?"

"'Teddy Bear' . . . ? No. It's been a long time since I've jumped rope." She sighed. "Haven't we talked about this enough, Jamie? There's nothing else to tell you about Bridget or Patrick and what happened to him. We won't speak of it again," she said with finality.

I knew she meant what she had said. I wouldn't get any more out of her. Maybe she didn't know why Bridget had done what she did. Maybe there was nothing else to learn from her.

To find out more, I needed another source.

CHAPTER 22

I glanced at the clock on my phone. The morning had passed, and no Sam. Numbness had crept into the center of my chest. I wasn't hungry. How could I eat when I had no idea where Sam was? I perused the refrigerator food Doug Moyer had relocated. Nothing was appetizing.

It would do me no good to stay here in the cabin. I'd go crazy waiting in the silence, wondering where Queenie was and where Sam had gone. I grabbed an apple and my purse.

I would drive Sam's truck into Bartlesville to visit the newspaper office and the genealogy library. The day would pass. Maybe when I returned, Sam would be here at the cabin.

Outside, I scanned the park area, still hoping to see Sam or Queenie. Instead, Betty Wood bustled across the lawn.

"Hello! How are you, dear? Is Sam back?"

"Not yet."

"Oh, I'm so surprised. Where can he be?" She considered the surrounding grounds, her eyes wide.

Sudden dislike stabbed my gut.

"Still no idea?" Betty frowned. "You don't suppose he's gotten cold feet about the marriage, do you?"

My jaw dropped. I hardly knew this woman. It was unbelievable she would say something so ridiculous. I wanted to slap her. I turned toward the truck. "No cold feet. I know Sam well enough to be certain of that."

"But no message, no phone call? Doesn't that bother you?" She followed me.

"Of course it bothers me. But I know Sam. He'll be back soon, or I'll hear from him with an explanation." I reached for the truck's door handle.

Betty took in my purse and the car keys in my hand. "You're headed out somewhere? If you're going by the park office, I could use a ride. I want to talk with them about a refund. Bernie and I may leave early."

I bit my tongue. Betty was annoying, but my southern upbringing had taught me not to be rude. "Hop in."

Betty chatted through the short drive, but I was too angry with her to listen. Besides, my head was full of Sam. If she asked me a question, I didn't hear it.

At the park office, a receptionist—whose nametag said: 'Karen'—was at her desk, typing on her computer.

"If Bernie and I leave early, can we get a refund?" Betty asked as she stepped up to the receptionist.

"Something wrong?" Karen pulled back from the keyboard and focused on Betty.

"As if a dead body and a smoke-filled cabin aren't enough?" Betty retorted. "We haven't completely decided. We're considering the option."

"We have a no-refund policy unless a waiting list for accommodations exists. Don't usually have a waitlist for midweek nights. Sorry."

"I can't believe it." Betty stiffened and stepped toward the door, then stopped in front of the brochure rack and reached for a pamphlet.

Karen greeted me with a weak smile. "You're Jamie Aldrich, right? Is cabin two okay? Mr. Snyder mentioned first thing today that he wanted to talk to you if you stopped by. I'll let him know you're here."

"Sure. I'll talk to him. And while I'm here, I'd like to see your group camp records. My mother was a counselor here back in the fifties. Do you have files for those years?"

"I seriously doubt it. You might check in that old file cabinet in the break room where Mr. Blunt's been working. Check the bottom drawer." She picked up her phone and pushed a button, then spoke. "Jamie Aldrich is here. She's headed for the break room." Karen smiled at me as she replaced the receiver. "He'll be out in a minute. Go ahead and flip through the files. Mr. Blunt won't be coming in to work on his research until mid-afternoon. He's in a rush to finish by the end of the week and move on to another park."

The outside office door slammed, and when I glanced around, Betty Wood was gone.

In the break room, an old green three-drawer filing cabinet sat in one corner, the battered top covered by loose files held down by a three-hole punch and a heavy-duty stapler. I scooted one of the chairs around so that I could sit while thumbing through the folders. Moving from front to back, I flipped through those in the lower drawer. They were crammed into the drawer in chronological order—one for every year back to 1960. I pulled open the middle drawer, then the top drawer, but found no more group camp files in the cabinet.

"Ms. Aldrich, I'm glad you stopped in," Roy Snyder said from the doorway to his office. "While we were searching for Mr. Mazie, the fire inspector went through the cabin. No other reason for the smoke was found other than those smoke bombs under the kitchen sink."

I still could not imagine who would light a smoke bomb in our cabin—or why.

"Still no Sam?" Snyder asked.

I shook my head and gestured toward the bottom drawer of the file cabinet. "I'm interested in the group camp. There are no records in the drawer for the years before 1960. Do you know where those files might be?"

"Stuffed in a box somewhere, if they still exist. What exactly were you looking for?"

"In 1954, my mother was a counselor here. So was the young man who fell from the cliff at the group camp overlook."

"I know the story, but not the specifics. Del Hilbert used to talk about that incident. He might have known your mother." Snyder scratched his head.

"Is there some way I could get in touch with him?"

"Not likely. He used to come out here a lot after he retired, but we haven't seen him for several weeks now. I understand he has a daughter lives up in Wyoming. Suppose he's up there."

"Where might the older group camp files be?"

Snyder shrugged. "You got me. Del might have sent them to Oklahoma City to be scanned digitally. I can give you a number to call." He stepped into his office and returned quickly with a business card. "Call this number. Tell them I referred you. They ought to be able to tell you something." He started to duck back into his office, then stopped. "Let me know when Sam gets back. Meanwhile, the rangers are watching for him. Are you going to file a missing person's report?"

Chill air dropped over me. Twenty-four hours with no word from Sam? Surely not. I swallowed. "I'll get back with you about that. There's something else I wanted to ask about," I said. Since my conversation with Mother, I'd been wondering. "Are there any funeral arrangements planned for Bridget? I'd like to meet her relatives and attend the service."

"A funeral? For a hermit?" Snyder leaned against the door-frame and crossed his arms. "I doubt it. Not even sure who the next of kin would be. I'm sure the sheriff would make the notification, and it would be up to family to decide. Why don't you check with Standingbear?"

CHAPTER 23

Back in Sam's truck, I headed out of the park. At the entrance, I flicked on the blinker and turned left onto the highway, the opposite direction from Bartlesville.

Stephen. He kept coming to mind. If anyone had come to the cabin after Sam last night, it would have been Stephen. Sam might be at his home, with him. Thinking he was there didn't ease my mind. It didn't explain why he hadn't called to check in with me and explain his absence.

As Sam and I had come to the park last week, he had pointed down a side road off the highway, telling me that Stephen lived about a mile and a half farther down the gravel road. I wished I had a map to pinpoint the exact location or that I had a newer vehicle with a navigation system. Without one, I could only drive in what I hoped was the correct direction.

A few miles down the highway, a county road sign indicated another street. I turned onto the gravel road and dropped the truck's speed down to twenty. Dust billowed in plumes behind the truck.

I slowed at each mailbox, watching for the name *Knapp*. Finally, there it was. I turned in at the drive and pulled up to a blue clapboard house with a grassy front yard. Small petunias, snapdragons, and other annual bloomers lifted their colorful heads in the breeze. The front door opened and a woman stepped out to stand at the top of the steps, her hand raised to shade her eyes from the intense afternoon sun. Thin, with prematurely gray hair pulled into a ponytail at the nape of her neck, she looked to be about my age. A red bandana was tied around her head.

"Can I help you?" She picked at the pocket of her jeans with one hand, then smoothed the fabric of her pink T-shirt.

"I'm Jamie Aldrich, Sam Mazie's fiancée. Are you Cindy?" I asked as I eased out of the truck. She gave a brief nod, and I walked toward the house. "Are Stephen and Sam here?"

"No. Haven't seen them." She leaned against the front porch railing, still shading her eyes.

I put one foot on the bottom step and started up. "Sam left last night and hasn't come back. I think he might be with your husband."

She stared at me, wide-eyed, as I reached the porch. "Stephen left last night, too." She touched her throat with her fingertips. "It's because of Bridget Halsted, isn't it?"

Halsted. I made a mental note of her last name. No one else had ever used it when referring to her. I could investigate her family in Bartlesville when I made it to the library.

"Stephen is a suspect in her death," I clarified.

Her hand dropped. "Bridget's dead?" Her pale face lost all its remaining color.

"Yes. She was found at the park last Friday morning."

Cindy's left hand fisted, and she turned to glance at the house.

"Can we talk for a minute? Please?" I asked.

She blinked. "What? The baby's sleeping. But, yes. Come in." She held the screen door open for me.

I entered the house. Braided rugs covered the floor. Animal figurines, faded wood signs, and bright quilted pillows had been placed throughout the room. Cindy sat on the sofa and pulled an afghan over her lap. Overhead, a ceiling fan circulated cool air. Down the hallway, tinkling music played a lullaby.

"I met Stephen on Friday. Sam and I were hoping the two

of you could join us for dinner sometime this week while we were at the park," I said as I dropped into a nearby chair.

"I doubt that will happen now." Cindy picked at the afghan. When she glanced up, her eyes had reddened. "They'll arrest Stephen once they find out about the money. They'll think he killed her for it. That's why he needed Sam's help."

"What money?"

"The gangsters' loot."

"Gangsters' loot? You've lost me. Doug Moyer told us a ghost story Saturday night about Pretty Boy Floyd and his gang. Are you saying the story is true?"

Cindy nodded. "I don't know exactly what Moyer said, but there is gangster money at the park. Stephen thinks it's buried at the apiary. He learned about it from that researcher who's writing a book."

"Aiden Blunt?"

"That's his name. He's been out here already today looking for Stephen."

Gangsters' loot buried at the apiary. The Bee Water emblem carved into the rock. X marks the spot. "Did Bridget know money had been buried there?"

"Stephen asked Bridget about it and she got angry. Said it belonged to her and that in a legal battle, she would have had first claim to the apiary."

I sat back, stunned. It was true. The gangsters had a hideout in the area, which had become a state park in the late thirties. The odd symbol, two wavy lines, was also carved on the bricks at the site of the old dilapidated wall.

"Bee Water," I said. Cindy's head jerked and her eyes widened.

"You know?"

I nodded. I knew now.

"If Bridget's dead, she can't claim the money and we can have it. We need it to pay for my chemo." She sniffed.

I averted my eyes from the kerchief tied around her head.

Stephen's actions on the day we met had new meaning now. I had wondered if he and Cindy were having marital problems, but it was an entirely different issue they were dealing with.

"Do you think they went to dig up the money?"

She shrugged. "I don't know. Stephen left late last night, after that awful storm. He said he'd be right back, but he never came home. I was hoping, when I saw the dust rising up from the road, that it was him."

Stephen had come to talk to Sam last night. Where were they now?

She laid her hands open in her lap and shut her eyes. "I'm so tired. Before you came, the sheriff was here, too, probably looking for Stephen. I didn't answer the door. I didn't want to tell him about the money."

"I don't know what the sheriff wanted with Stephen. It might have nothing to do with Bridget."

"Bridget was crazy, you know, always ranting at Stephen about not doing this or that correctly at the hives. And then she was the one that got stung and nearly died. She would have died, if Stephen hadn't driven her to the hospital." Cindy fell back against the sofa cushions. "I'm just so tired."

"Can I get you something before I go?"

Her head flopped back and forth against the sofa cushions. "No. I don't need anything." She opened her eyes. "I wish you the best life with Sam. Tell him I said so." She pulled her legs up beneath her on the sofa and threw the afghan over them.

I let myself out.

In the truck, I started the engine but continued to sit in the driveway. Wherever he was, Sam was with Stephen. There was immense relief in knowing that, but I couldn't deny the rising anger I felt. Phone or no phone, why had neither of them contacted their loved ones? What were they doing? I had to also assume that Queenie was with them. I closed my eyes and took a few deep breaths. Boy, did I have some things to talk to Sam about.

He would be at the cabin when I got back. He might even be there now. I blew out a deep breath. The muscles in my back, which had been rigid with apprehension and fear, relaxed.

I still had a couple of errands to run in Bartlesville. It would do Sam good to wonder where I was for a change.

CHAPTER 24

I made the short drive east to Bartlesville and parked outside the library, then sat for a minute in the parking lot, reviewing what I wanted to research there: Patrick Gallagher the elder and Patrick Gallagher the younger, the one who had loved my mother. Thanks to Cindy, I now knew Bridget's last name and could research the Halsted family.

Once inside, I went straight to the librarian. After telling her what I was hoping to find, she pointed me toward the research section and suggested a few volumes, including the Washington County censuses and a book called *Washington County Families.* I settled in with the books, searching for information on Patrick Gallagher.

An hour later, I pushed those books and three others away from me and sat back. Among the Gallaghers listed were Patrick, husband; Claudine, wife; and Patrick, a son, who was listed as twelve years old in the 1950 census. In 1960, Claudine was listed as a widow and head of household with another child who was listed as 'foster'; she was absent from the 1970 census. I reviewed a few phone books and business directories but found no other Gallagher listings.

I checked the census books for my own family, the Jamisons, and found my grandparents in the census listings for 1930, 1940, and 1950. The latter two included mention of my mother, a daughter, living at home.

Next, I searched for Bridget Halsted. I found her listed as

a member of the family of Charles and Doreen Halsted in the 1940 and 1950 censuses for the town of Dewey. In the 1960 and 1970 censuses, she was listed as a resident of Bartlesville employed as a teacher. Her name wasn't listed in the 1980 Oklahoma census.

I slid my notes into my purse, thanked the librarian, and went back out to the truck.

My third errand took me to the south part of Bartlesville and the newspaper office, where I asked to review the archives for 1954. The staff member in charge of the newspaper morgue was a woman too young to remember anything that had happened that summer—she hadn't yet been born. I selected the microfiche spools from July and August of 1954 and scooted into the chair in front of a microfiche machine.

I threaded the machine with the end of the film and pushed the *forward* button. Once the picture of a newspaper page appeared, I focused the screen. It didn't take long to find the newspaper article reporting the accident. It was a bulletin on the front page.

Camp Counselor Falls to His Death

A counselor at the Osage Hills State Park group camp has fallen to his death, according to Elliot Davis, park manager. The incident is under investigation and details are not yet available. The name of the victim has not been released.

I used the *'forward'* switch to advance the machine's film reel to the next day's issue and found no mention of the death. Two days later, another article appeared.

Local Boy Dies in Fall from State Park Cliff

Patrick Gallagher, 18, died Monday after falling from a cliff above Sand Creek in Osage Hills State Park. Galla-

gher, who was working at the camp as a summer coun-
selor, died at the site from injuries sustained in the fall.

According to Elliot Davis, park manager, Gallagher
was a well-liked counselor with many friends. Report-
edly, several counselors had been "horsing around"
on the cliff the previous evening. Davis speculates that
after park officials interrupted the horseplay, Gallagher
returned alone and fell to his death. The death has been
ruled accidental.

Gallagher is survived by his father, Patrick, his
mother, Claudine, and sister, Pauline, of the Bartlesville
home.

I studied the high school photograph of Patrick. Something
about him seemed familiar. He reminded me of someone, but
who? I returned the microfiche reel to the file drawer. The
story was the same as the one my mother told. Simple and
tragic. Case closed.

In the back of my mind, the possibility that Sam might
be waiting for me at the cabin in the park hovered. If he was
there, he would call, wouldn't he?

I had one more bit of research to do at the newspaper office.

"Could you tell me if you have any articles noted about
Bridget Halsted?" I asked the newspaper staffer.

She sat down at the morgue's computer. "Spell it."

I did, and she typed the name into the computer's search
engine.

Three stories popped up on the screen, each with a date
and a brief summary. The first was a high school graduation
article from 1954, the second a story about an eighth grade
science class and a field trip to the Woolaroc Museum and
Park in 1969, and the third a story about beekeeping at Osage
Hills State Park from 1996, five years ago.

I returned to the microfiche drawers and found the reels

with the correct date ranges. Then I went back to the machine I'd been using, threaded the film and searched for the first article.

The first story was one of several featured in that issue concerning the graduation of Bridget's high school class, where, as valedictorian, she had given a speech at the ceremony. She was also listed as the class vice president and was a member of several societies at the school. My mother had told me the truth about Bridget's popularity and her intelligence. So why had she become a hermit? I rethreaded the reel and inserted the second.

That news story was a picture. It showed a teacher and her class during a field trip to Woolaroc Museum, the country estate of Frank Phillips, founder of Phillips Petroleum, which houses eclectic items from around the world. Bridget, the teacher, smiled into the camera, wearing glasses with thick frames, her dark hair in a pageboy. She was identified as a fifth grade teacher and the sponsor of the elementary school's science club. Again, I hit the rewind button, and when the film had rewound, I pulled it off the machine and inserted the third microfiche film reel.

The photo at the top of the third story was of Stephen Knapp and Bridget. The article detailed how Stephen planned to expand his homegrown honey production business by adding the Bee Water honey company, which had operated for more than twenty years at Osage Hills State Park. His company would now incorporate the Bee Water name, originally coined by local beekeeper Bridget Halsted. In the photograph, Bridget's face was turned away from the camera, but even having seen her face only once, she was recognizable.

'I found you,' the jump rope rhyme note had said. Was this article the clue that had led someone to Bridget at Osage Hills State Park?

CHAPTER 25

My errands in Bartlesville had taken several hours. Now, my mind settled on Sam. Hope still lingered that he would be waiting for me at the cabin when I returned. Possibly, the ordeal I'd been going through for the past fourteen hours would end. I could imagine how our reunion would go: he would be sorry for leaving me in the dark and I would pout a little, but not much; I would be too happy to act otherwise for more than a minute. But an undercurrent of anxiety still flowed through my body.

I pulled into the driveway of the cabin, jumped from the truck, and ran to unlock the door. The living room was empty. The bedroom was empty. My heart sank.

He might be waiting for me outside, on the picnic table. Of course that was it—he didn't yet have a key to the cabin.

I slid open the door to the empty patio. My heart took another dive. Anxiety rushed into my head, bringing along a headache. Why wasn't he here?

I dropped onto the picnic table bench and closed my eyes. My stomach turned over, and nausea rose up my throat. *Oh, Sam. Where are you?* I had a terrible feeling I might never see Sam alive again.

I grasped at straws. What if the note I had left at the other cabin had somehow blown away? What if Sam had no idea where I was and was waiting there, wondering when I'd show up?

I ran, heart pounding, across the mown lawn to the other ring of cabins and down the asphalt road to cabin seven. The street in front of the cabin and the driveway were empty. I tried the front doorknob; it was locked. I raced around the cabin. *Please be there, please be there*, I chanted in my head.

The back yard was empty. I leaned against the end of the picnic table and sucked air. It was hard to breathe when crying, especially after sprinting. I knelt at the end of the table, rocking back and forth. *My God, Sam. Where are you?*

Something cold touched my leg. I jerked and looked down. Big brown eyes gazed up at me.

"Woof," Queenie said.

I dropped to the ground and clutched the animal to me, not caring that she was muddy and covered in briars. She licked my salty tears and whined. The dog lifted her paw and nosed at it. I took her paw in my hand and gently probed it with my fingers, finally pulling a burr from between two of her toes. She yelped, then licked my hand and her paw. I checked her other feet for stickers and found several. I pulled even more from her belly and the ends of her ears. A few minutes later, confident I'd found all of the burrs, I held her close and petted her.

Although Queenie's short body hair had repelled most of the mud and not provided a place for the stickers to lodge, she needed a bath. I patted her head. She scooted close to me, laid her head on my thigh, and sighed. I stroked her, and within seconds, the dog was asleep.

"Where have you been, Queenie?" I asked the dog.

I remembered a night a year ago at Elizabeth's house in Pawhuska when the hound had whined at the backdoor, needing food and water. She had been a comfort, a companion, and a guardian during those weeks in Pawhuska.

I rubbed her ears, and she moaned.

"Oh, how I wish you could talk. Do you know where Sam is, Queenie? Do you?"

Without lifting her head, she opened her eyes and looked at me, then partially closed them again.

"You don't know, do you? You haven't been with Sam. You've been lost in the forest."

Queenie's tongue darted out and gave my jeans a lick.

"What happened to your collar? If you hadn't been smart enough to find your way back here, you might have been lost to us forever." I gathered the dog into my arms and pulled myself up. "Come on, girl. We've relocated. Let's go get you cleaned up before we have a long talk about what we need to do next."

After Queenie had been bathed and fed, I curled up on the sofa, the dog beside me and partially under the blanket that covered my legs. It was mid-afternoon on a warm May day, but I shivered. Despair settled over me like fog. I couldn't think of any way to get rid of it. Until Sam walked in that door, I didn't see it ever going away.

When Ben died, I had told myself not to expect to love again. I should be satisfied with having been completely in love twice—once with my college love, Rob, and once with Ben, years after my divorce. Who was I to expect to love someone enough to marry a third time? Finding Sam after being apart for thirty years and remembering the childhood crush we had shared had been a gift from God at a time I needed one.

I had been so happy when our mutual attraction turned into love, a little glimmer at first, and eventually a shining, growing entity that threated to burst my heart open. How could Sam be gone? How could our future be over in an instant? I closed my eyes and snuggled into Queenie.

In my head, a little blue ball began in a corner of my brain and began to grow larger, rolling its way to me. Words were written on the ball. *Bee Water.*

I sat up. Bee Water. Cindy had mentioned the apiary this morning. Maybe the men had gone there—and were still there—searching for the 'treasure' Cindy had mentioned. Maybe all I needed to do was go there to find them.

I threw off the blanket, grabbed Queenie's leash from the table, and snapped it around her neck like a collar. Together, we ran for the truck.

I drove too fast out of the cabin cul-de-sac and down the park's main road. At the RV camp, I turned right, following the asphalt to the old service road that led to the CCC camp. I parked the truck and hopped out with Queenie.

In the tent camping area, four teenagers were throwing Frisbees on a strip of green lawn by the restrooms. People lingered around several of the campsite grills, preparing to cook supper. Wood smoke billowed into the air from the blaze in the central fire pit. Two men lounged nearby in folding camp chairs, drinking beer.

As I headed for the old road, my steps slowed. It was stupid to think that Stephen and Sam would still be at the apiary now. If the pair had ever been there, it would have been last night. If they were here in the park, the rangers or the sheriff would surely have found them. That is, if they were still searching.

The campfire smoke followed me as I walked up the old road, reminding me of the smoke bombs in the kitchen. Had that happened only last night?

It made sense that Stephen had planted and lit the bombs. Beekeepers used smoke to subdue bees. He would have the equipment and the expertise to carry that off. What I didn't understand was the subterfuge.

The sun had dropped lower in the cloudless blue sky when I reached the ruins of the CCC camp. Two crows cawed as they flapped overhead, flying east. The still air was sticky with humidity. I turned west toward the apiary, tugging on Queenie's leash to keep her with me. The two of us walked down the center of the strip of meadow. I shaded my eyes from the sun and watched for movement as I neared the white bee boxes.

At the beginning of the tree line on one side of the meadow, I stopped. From this vantage point, I could see most of the hives. Nothing moved in the area. A pair of bees buzzed past on their way to a hive. I surveyed the meadow again. This time I noticed a figure sitting on a boulder near the rock where the Bee Water symbol had been carved. My heart lurched. The man waved.

Queenie and I cut across the meadow, stepping through grass that had already grown knee-high in the eight weeks since spring had begun.

Aiden Blunt stood. "What are you doing here?" he asked, frowning.

I searched for signs of disturbance that might indicate Stephen and Sam had been digging in their search for the loot.

"Looking for my fiancé. Have you seen Sam?"

Queenie sniffed around the boulders where Blunt sat.

"Nope. What makes you think he'd be here?"

"It's his cousin's apiary. He took it over from Bridget Halsted."

Blunt squinted at me. His mouth worked but he didn't speak. He brushed at his thinning hair with one hand. "What do you know about Bridget Halsted?"

Queenie responded to his angry tone with a low growl. The hair on the back of her neck bristled.

"Not much. You knew her, didn't you? Stephen's wife Cindy said you were the one who told Stephen about the gangsters' loot. And you were looking for him earlier today." I kept Queenie's leash tight. She watched the man as she leaned into my knee.

Blunt glanced at the sun. "Bridget knew all about the loot. She'd known since we were teenagers."

"Did you also know my mother, Mary Jamison?"

Blunt squinted at me. "Mary Jamison. Yes. I can see that. Is your mother still living?"

"In Rio Rancho, north of Albuquerque." I patted Queenie on the head. The dog sat on her haunches.

"She ever get back here?"

"Not since her parents died."

"Did she know Bridget was here?"

"I told her. She and Bridget didn't stay in touch after mom married my dad." I shifted my weight and relaxed a little. This was my chance to get Blunt to tell me something about Bridget.

Before I could ask any more questions, he bent down to brush some dirt off the toe of his hiking boot and said, "You have no claim to that treasure." Blunt glared at me.

"Why would I think I did?"

"Your mom knows where it is. So did Bridget." His face darkened. "She sent you after it, didn't she? You can tell her I'm the one who's going to dig it up. My father put it here. I'll be damned if anybody but me is going to retrieve it now."

Blunt's eye glistened with something wild. I'd seen it before, in another very intelligent acquaintance last fall who had wanted me dead.

"I don't want your treasure. And my mom doesn't want it, either." The list of things I wanted to talk to my mother about was growing by the minute. "But I think you need to consider sharing it with Stephen, since he has the apiary contract. That's the only right thing to do now that Bridget's gone." I remembered Aiden's reaction to the news of Bridget's death last Friday. If he'd been acting, he'd fooled me. Previously, his grief had been apparent. Now, I wasn't so sure.

"How would you know anything about what's 'right' by me?" he growled.

I shrugged, glancing at the meadow and the rolling woodlands and wishing I had not come alone.

"I thought Sam might be up here with Stephen. You haven't seen them, have you?" I asked softly, changing the subject in hopes of diffusing his anger.

"No." He wiped one hand across his eyes and sighed. His body slumped. "I spent most of the day at the CCC camp ruins. Taking pictures for my book."

"Karen told me this morning that you were finishing up here and moving on to the next site."

He blinked and his face faded to a normal color. "Yes."

"Aiden, I've been talking with my mother about Patrick Gallagher. You remember him?"

Now his face blanched and his eyed widened. "Wh—what about Patrick?"

"He and my mother dated. He carved their names on a wall out by an old gangster hideout."

"I don't want to talk about Patrick. His death was senseless. Tragic."

"Yes. It sounds like it was."

Aiden's shoulders slumped. "Life could have been so different." He looked up at the sky, unfocused.

I waited for a few minutes, until it was apparent his thoughts had gone elsewhere. "I'll go now. I can see that the men aren't here. If they show up, will you tell Sam I'll see him at the cabin?"

Blunt's chin dropped, and he collapsed onto the boulder again, his eyes still unfocused.

"Come on, Queenie. Let's go." I tugged her leash and hurried down the meadow, glancing at the shadows on either side.

The sun was dropping lower, but its rays still burned my skin. Queenie trotted to keep up. Both the ranger and the park manager had said they'd watch for Sam today. If he'd been in the park, one of them would have seen him. There might be good news at the cabin.

My stomach growled. Food had been the least of my worries today, but I was beginning to feel lightheaded. And anxious. The closer we got to the twenty-four-hour mark of Sam's disappearance, the more worried I was becoming.

Please, Sam, be at the cabin.

CHAPTER 26

I opened the cabin door to emptiness and heartbreaking silence.

My earlier feeling of hunger had disappeared. I fed Queenie and then spread peanut butter and jelly on a slice of bread before trudging outside to the picnic table with the bread and a bottle of beer. The sun had dropped below the trees, and the peaceful pink-gray light of evening fell like snowflakes over the park.

The sandwich caught in my throat and I took swallows of beer to wash it down. Voices carried on the breeze from the cabins across the way, where families lingered outside after cooking out on their grills. Had I still been at the other cabin, Bernard and Betty would no doubt have come over to keep me company once they saw me sitting outside. I did not know the neighbors in the cabin next to me now.

The hair on my forearms prickled. I was being watched. Solitude, which I usually enjoyed, turned to terror. I grabbed the remains of my dinner from the table and hurried into the cabin, then locked the door.

Inside, I closed the living room curtain, piled logs into the fireplace, and started a fire, even though I knew my shivering had nothing to do with being cold. Queenie huddled with me on the sofa.

My cell phone rang. I wanted so badly for it to be Sam. I hated not knowing where he was. My stomach twisted inside me as it digested the bit of sandwich I'd just eaten. I grabbed the phone, not immediately recognizing the number listed on the caller ID.

"Hello?" My voice croaked.

"Jamie? I thought you were bringing Queenie home tonight. I miss her." Trudy's voice quivered.

"Oh, sweetie. I'm sorry." I'd forgotten about returning the dog to my cousin today, mostly because Queenie had been gone for half of the time she'd been allotted to spend with us. I couldn't bear to part with her while Sam was still missing. And that meant telling Trudy the truth, that I didn't have a clue where Sam was. She would be upset. I reminded myself that Trudy was an adult, and despite what some people thought, she was intelligent and able to handle whatever bad news I shared.

"Are you bringing her now?"

"Trudy, something's come up. It may be tomorrow. Can you stand it without her for one more day? I can't get away from the park tonight." I sighed. "Sam's not here, and I need Queenie with me."

"But I miss her. She keeps me safe. This house is too big."

"Isn't Aunt Elizabeth there with you?" I asked. "And Vera could come over."

"My Liz is here. But Queenie makes me feel safe when I'm asleep. Where is Sam?"

If my heart had not already been aching, it was now. Where *was* Sam? I'd been asking that question for nearly twenty-four hours. A knot grew in my throat. "I don't know where he is. And I'm worried. I'd like to keep Queenie tonight. Maybe Sam will be back tomorrow."

"You don't know where Sam is? He should be there. What about the wedding planning?"

"There's no planning going on here. Trudy, ask Vera to come over. Just for tonight."

"But what if Sam doesn't come back tomorrow? I want to talk to him. He should be there with you."

I glanced around the empty cabin. What could I say to that? He wasn't here, and I didn't have a clue where he was.

"I'll call you tomorrow, okay?" I petted the dog's smooth fur and scratched her favorite spots. Her right hind leg jerked. "Call Vera. Okay?"

"I guess," Trudy grumbled. "But I miss Queenie. And I miss you. I'm mad at Sam."

"I miss you, too. See you soon!" I hung up on that cheery note, pressing the *off* button even though there was a chance Trudy wasn't finished talking with me yet. I clutched the phone to my chest and said a prayer. *Please let Sam be okay.*

I cuddled with the dog on the sofa for a minute, feeling sorry for myself. I was tempted to open another bottle of beer or drink a glass of wine, but drinking alone had no appeal. I had to do something constructive. I wasn't sleepy, and although the sun had set and the light was fading from the sky outside the living room's picture window, it was way too early to call it a night. And in the Mountain Time Zone, where Mother lived, the sun was still above the western horizon.

I organized my thoughts and grabbed my cell phone again to punch in the familiar number.

"Mother," I said when she answered on the fourth ring, "can we talk a little more about Bridget and that summer? Please?"

"Jamie, I told you the subject was closed. I don't want to talk about it." Her voice had that hard tone she seemed to always have when we talked.

"What really happened that night?"

My mother breathed into the phone. "You're not going to drop this, are you?"

"No, I'm not. Sam is missing. I'm beginning to think Bridget might have been murdered, Mom. And what's happened to Sam may be related to her death." My voice quivered. "Please, Mom, I want to find Sam. Can you help?"

"Sam's missing?" she said in a low voice. "Oh, my God." She sniffed. "I don't see how the two things could be related."

She paused and I could hear her breathing. Finally, she continued, "We were kids. None of us had any idea ..." Her voice trailed off.

"Any idea about what, Mom?"

"How dangerous walking on the edge of the overlook was, or anything else we did that summer! Tempting fate. So stupid. We thought we were invincible. You remember feeling that way, don't you?"

"Of course." Experience had taught me that the feeling didn't go away until you were faced with a life-and-death situation. "Maybe if I tell you what I know . . ."

"I can't promise anything."

"I know Bridget's last name was Halsted. There is a researcher here who knew her, and who knew you back in the day. His name is Aiden Blunt. And he told me today that both you and Bridget knew about some loot hidden by some gangsters back in the thirties."

"Aiden Blunt." She bit off the words. "He's there, too?"

"He's researching a book on the CCC camps in Oklahoma. He's leaving on Friday."

"Was he at the park when Bridget died?" Her voice seemed to come from much farther away than Rio Rancho.

"Yes. We saw him that morning not long after the ranger, Sam, and I found the body." My mind connected bits and pieces of what I knew. "Did Patrick know about the buried loot, too? Did his death have something to do with the money?"

"How was Sam involved in this? Why would you think what's happened to him has anything to do with Bridget?"

My throat tightened. I would give anything to believe there was a simpler explanation for Sam's absence. I might be clutching at straws, but it was all I had.

"Jamie Lynn? Was everything good between you and Sam before he left?"

Leave it to my mother to read something into my silence. I sniffed. "Yes."

"You are lying. I have always been able to tell when you

were lying. It's not working out, is it? Being hundreds of miles apart was easy compared to the everyday business of having a relationship, isn't it?"

"Everything was fine with the two of us. Something happened in the middle of the night Sunday at our cabin: smoke in the kitchen, but no fire. He disappeared during the incident."

"But that was an entire day ago. You haven't heard from him?"

I rested my head on the table. I didn't want to talk about this. My stomach hurt, my head hurt, my heart hurt.

"Can we get back to the reason I called? Tell me what you were doing the night before Patrick fell."

"Oh, Jamie. It's been so long . . ." She paused. Ice clinked in a glass.

I sat up, closing my eyes and hoping she would continue with the story and tell me the truth.

She swallowed and sighed, then began again. "It was a double date, the last Friday before the final group of summer campers headed home on Saturday. I was with Patrick. Bridget was with Bernie."

Bernie? The same Bernie who was here now, at the park? I pressed the phone closer to my ear.

"We were . . . at the overlook at the group camp. Patrick, Del, Aiden, and Bernie started horsing around, showing off for us girls, Bridget and a couple of others." Her voice broke. "I'm still not sure what happened."

"What was Bernie's last name, Mom?" I asked the question even though I knew the answer. All of them had been here that night, the night Patrick fell. And they were here now.

"My memories are so foggy. How can so many years have passed?"

Her voice faded. I waited.

"Oh, I don't know. Bernie . . . Bernie Wood! That's it. He was flirting with two girls at the camp. Bridget, and the other one was—let me think. Betty. I didn't know her, but she was mad about Bernie's date with Bridget. So silly. It was all so silly. She and Del hung around with us even though we hadn't included them in our plans."

"Was it Del Hilbert, Mom?" My swirling thoughts came together. My mom had been at the cliff all those years ago.

"Ye-es. How did you know?"

Del Hilbert had been the park manager who allowed Bridget to live here in the park, according to Snyder. Had he known he was helping her hide? I squeezed my eyes closed and tried to imagine the scenario that last night, before Patrick fell.

"Did Patrick walk you back to your cabin?"

"No. We went alone."

"And neither of you went out again?"

"Jamie, that's all I remember. If there was anything else . . . What about Sam? How could any of this help find Sam?"

I tried to focus. My brain felt scrambled. I had no idea if anything Mother knew could help me find Sam. My mother had known Patrick Gallagher, Bridget, Del Hilbert, Aiden Blunt, and even Betty and Bernard Wood. It couldn't be a coincidence they were all part of this park's history. The coincidence was that I was here, in my mother's stead, and that Bernard, Betty and Aiden were visiting the park.

"You'll keep me posted about Sam, won't you? Call tomorrow."

I hung up the phone after agreeing to call in the afternoon or as soon as I learned anything new. I walked around the cabin, making sure all the doors and windows were locked. Queenie padded along behind me, her toes clicking on the painted cement floors. I took a shower and crawled into bed.

Something nagged at me, buzzing in my head. I had told Aiden Blunt today that my mother was Mary Jamison. And if I remembered correctly, I had mentioned her to Betty and Bernard on Saturday night when they'd joined us for dinner.

Why would they deliberately hide the fact that they'd known my mother so long ago?

My mind jumped to another possibility. Aiden had acted suspicious of me when I'd told him who I was. Distrust of me meant distrust of Sam, didn't it? We were obviously together, a team—and possibly a threat to something that was happening here at the park, now. Maybe Bridget's death had only been the beginning.

CHAPTER 27

Tuesday, May 21

I pulled the bedroom curtains open and met with a drizzly, gray day. I had hoped for sunshine, something to lift my spirits as I continued my search for my fiancé. It was not to be.

"Queenie?"

The dog's nails scratched on the floor as she wiggled her way out from under the bed. I dropped down onto the floor and hugged the dog to me. She whined and licked my cheek before struggling away and scurrying toward her food bowl in the kitchen.

I folded into a ball on the floor. *Sam? Where are you?*

Queenie woofed. Someone rapped lightly on the cabin's front door.

I rushed to the door, forgetting that I was wearing my nightshirt and had not even yet brushed my teeth. I slipped off the chain latch and threw the door wide.

"Morning, Jamie. I'm sorry it's so early." Sheriff John Standingbear looked past me into the living room. "I need to talk to you. I have some information."

I wrapped my arms around myself. "Excuse me a minute." I closed the door and raced for the bedroom, pulled on my clothes and quickly brushed my teeth. When I returned to the porch of the cabin, the sheriff was on his phone, leaning against the cabin's front wall.

He held up a finger at me as he finished his conversation. After he slipped his phone back into the case attached to his belt, he stepped past me through the open door and into the cabin.

"Still no word from Sam?" he asked.

"No. And you haven't found anything in the park?"

"I'm sorry to say we have not. However, I spoke with Stephen's wife, Cindy, last night. She said Stephen was missing, too. That he had left home Sunday night to meet Sam." He watched for my reaction.

"I talked to Cindy yesterday and she told me the same thing. But I still haven't heard from Sam."

"Evidently, Sam left voluntarily and is not in harm's way."

His eyes told me he was sorry. I didn't like feeling pitied. Heaviness fell over my body. I wanted nothing more than to crawl back in bed and cover my head with the quilt. This nightmare was not going to end.

"Sam wouldn't do that to me." My lip trembled.

"I don't believe he would either, but the facts as we have them now tell a different story." He half-turned toward the door, but stopped. "There is something else you might like to know, even though it has nothing to do with Sam."

"What?" I leaned against the wall by the door, my hand on the handle.

"The autopsy came back on Bridget Halsted. The medical examiner made note of something interesting. One of the things they look at is lividity."

I was familiar with the word which had to do with the way blood pools in body tissues immediately after death, coagulating at the body's lowest points. "I know the term."

"And you also might have noticed that Bridget's face had a mottled bruise on one cheek."

I nodded. "Actually, I did notice that, but I didn't connect it to lividity."

"Neither did we, at first. But the ME says otherwise. The shape and pattern of that bruise indicate that Bridget was lying on top of the branch when she died, when her blood settled. Timing-wise, the ME thinks she died of the head wound while in the tree and that her body eventually dropped to the ground. The branch fell on top of her several hours later. He places the time of death at one a.m. Friday morning, probably during the storm we had that night."

I tried to process what he was telling me. Bridget had climbed the tree with a head wound and eventually died there?

"Bridget was murdered," he said grimly. "The falling tree had nothing to do with her death. But it made a good cover-up for a few days. Our investigation into the event is now a full-blown murder investigation. Anyone still in the park who was here last Thursday or Friday will be interviewed before they leave. I've instructed that roadblocks be set up."

I nodded, considering all the implications of what he had just told me.

"You know we had some questions for Stephen, Jamie, even before we knew Bridget was murdered. The two of them had business dealings and were seen arguing. Most recently, just last Wednesday. He's now officially a person of interest. When they are found, Stephen may be arrested and Sam could be accused of aiding and abetting."

"But Sam wouldn't do that. You know him, Sheriff."

"People do strange things when they're in trouble."

As I shut the door behind the sheriff, my hands shook. Sam had left voluntarily. Sam was staying away voluntarily. He was not missing; he was AWOL from my life.

I sank onto the sofa, resting my head on my hands. The Sam I knew would not have done this. The Sam I knew would not have left me to wonder where he was and what he was doing. The Sam I knew would know exactly how hard this would be on me, that my trust in him would be forever damaged.

What had happened?

Queenie padded in from the kitchen and sat in front of me. She rested her big head on my knee and stared up with her soulful brown eyes. Her tail thumped the floor. I patted her head and burst into tears.

Some time later, tears spent, I snapped Queenie's leash around her neck and loaded her into Sam's truck. I couldn't sit in the cabin all day, moping about Sam and wondering if I had done something to drive him away. I didn't like the other thought that occurred to me any better. If it wasn't something I had done, was it the loot he and Stephen had found after Stephen killed Bridget?

I was thinking ridiculous thoughts. I needed to keep my mind off Sam, at least for the time being.

I drove the park's asphalt road to the group camp, to the overlook where Patrick Gallagher had died. If he hadn't died that night, would a relationship have bloomed with my mother? Would she and my father have ever met?

Three white trucks were parked haphazardly outside the camp meeting hall. Painting paraphernalia, drop cloths, and stacked cans of paint cluttered the beds of the pickups. I parked and walked with Queenie past the vehicles and around the building to the overlook. Once there, I peered down at the creek below, where white water churned between limestone boulders. The rush of the water filled my head like white noise.

The ledge was uneven with only a single braided cable preventing a fall of 50 feet to the creek. I could imagine teenage boys tempting death by walking the edge. I couldn't imagine why Patrick would have returned here alone, long after the others had gone to bed. He fell to his death. People assumed it had been an accident, just as we had assumed Bridget's death had been an accident. Could Patrick, like Bridget, have been murdered?

A low growl rumbled in Queenie's throat.

"Quite a drop, isn't it?" A low voice asked.

Bernard Wood crossed the concrete patio to stand beside me. He gazed over the edge and moved back. "You don't have a death wish, do you? Thought you were getting married." He frowned as he studied my face. "Sam hasn't come back, has he? Any word from him?"

I shook my head. Queenie's growl continued to rumble although she sat quietly at my right side.

"Sorry. That has to be tough to take."

What I really wanted was someone to spill my heart out to about how horrible this feeling was, how I didn't know whether to be worried about Sam's safety or angry because he'd left me behind. I searched Bernie's face and found that his eyes were blank; in fact, the look in them made me wonder if he was sorry at all.

I kept my mouth shut and looked over the edge again.

"I'm wondering about the young man who died here back in 1954," I said. "His name was Patrick Gallagher. There was a question about him Sunday night after Aiden Blunt's speech. You and Betty were already gone."

Bernard huffed. "Aiden Blunt. Wouldn't listen to him, if I were you. The man's a detestable fake."

"He seems nice, and sincerely interested in the CCC camp research."

"It's a cover. In fact, his whole life is one big cover-up."

"Why do you say that?"

"Yes, my dear. The question is 'Why?' Why now? Blunt here, at this place, at this time, with his history? You want to hear a good story, you should ask him about Patrick Gallagher. But I doubt he'd tell you the truth." Bernard picked up a pebble and pitched it over the cliff.

"Will you tell me the truth?"

"About what?" He tossed a larger stone.

"Bridget. My mother told me the two of you dated that summer, with her and Patrick."

I let my words soak in. Bernard studied the ground.

"I wouldn't say we 'dated.' That implies both parties were in it. Bridget had eyes for someone else."

"And Betty had eyes for you."

"Your mother told you that, did she? I wonder what else she's told you." He stuffed his hands in his pockets and swayed on his heels.

"Not much. A lot of years have passed. She hardly remembers anything."

"Humph." Bernard pulled one hand out of his pocket and smoothed his hair. Seconds later, he cleared his throat. "So you say." He marched away.

Queenie stood to watch him go.

I lingered at the overlook, watching the waters of the creek spill over the rocks below, but staying a safe distance from the edge. I wondered what Betty and Bernard would say when they were interviewed as they left the park. I couldn't see either of them as murderers, but that meant nothing. Murderers didn't advertise their escapades or their thoughts, as I knew from experience.

Bernard clearly did not like Aiden. And it had nothing to do with jealousy from long ago. I would talk to my mother again today. She might remember something more about the night Patrick Gallagher had died, something that would explain why all of these people were here, in the park, at the time Bridget was murdered.

Could I ask the right questions in such a way that she would tell me what I wanted to know about Bridget, Patrick, and even Aiden?

CHAPTER 28

The morning sun was trying without success to burn through the gray clouds as Queenie and I walked to Sam's truck. My stomach roiled and worry throbbed in my temples. A gnat buzzed around my face; another buzzed inside my brain. What had happened between Bernard and Aiden? Did it have something to do with Bridget, or Patrick, or someone else within their teenage group fifty years ago?

At the cabin, Queenie trotted ahead of me and wagged her tail as I unlocked the door. I stopped in the living room and dropped my keys and pack on the table. Queenie continued into the kitchen. Nose to the bottom of the back door, she growled and barked, hair raised in a ridge along her back. I knew the dog's habits well enough to know that something was at the back door, or on the patio.

Without a peephole or window in the door, it was impossible to tell who—or what—was at the door without opening it. A raccoon? Or Sam? My heart leapt into my throat. I left the chain lock in place, unlocked the knob, and opened the door a crack.

Queenie continued to growl and bark. Through the crack, I could see someone lying in front of the door. My heart raced as I fumbled to unlatch the chain so I could jerk the door open. A man with dark hair in a filthy blue T-shirt, dirt-encrusted jeans, and muddy boots lay in a fetal position at my feet.

"Sam?" I gasped. I knelt and gently turned the face to the

light. Not Sam. Stephen. I felt for a pulse in his neck and found it. His cool skin was a grayish-pink, and his face was smeared with mud and bits of green leaves. A wound on the side of his head seeped blood. Several insect bites had welted up on his cheeks and forehead.

"Stephen, can you hear me? Wake up." I pulled at his arms and patted his face. He groaned and stirred. I patted him again. Queenie quieted but stood next to me, her long tail wagging slowly back and forth as I worked. When Stephen didn't respond, I dashed into the cabin, grabbed the quilt off the sofa, and threw it over his body.

"I'm going to call for help. Hang on, Stephen."

I ran back inside and called 911 with my cell phone, told the dispatcher the emergency and my location, then returned to the back door. I tucked the quilt underneath Stephen, rolling his body from side to side as I shoved the material under him, then dragged him into the kitchen. I shook him and patted his cheeks, trying to rouse him.

Queenie whined. I wetted a dishcloth and swabbed Stephen's face. "Stephen. Wake up. It's Jamie. You're going to be all right. Wake up."

I continued to swab his face and talk to him until, a few minutes later, the dog trotted to the front door. A knock came. I ran to the front door.

"Ms. Aldrich, 9-1-1 dispatch called the park. The ambulance is on the way out from Bartlesville," Park Manager Snyder said when I pulled the door open. "What's wrong?"

"Sam's cousin Stephen is here. I got home a few minutes ago and found him at the back door. He's unconscious."

Snyder glanced over my shoulder and into the cabin. "Where's Sam?"

"Not here." I stepped aside to let Snyder in and gestured toward the kitchen. "Stephen was alone." Leaving the front door open, I followed him to the kitchen.

He knelt to check Stephen's pulse as I had. "Any visible wounds?"

"On the side of his head. He's pale and his breathing is shallow. I think he's in shock."

A siren's wail pierced the air. A minute later, EMTs rushed into the cabin and started work on Stephen, checking his vital signs and assessing his injuries. One of them spoke on a radio to the hospital, then inserted an IV. When they carried Stephen on a gurney to the ambulance, Snyder and I followed through the front door to stand on the lawn.

"Someone should go with him. And Cindy, his wife, needs to know," I said.

"You call Cindy. I'll follow the ambulance into town. I expect Standingbear is on his way here now. He'll have heard about this from dispatch, too."

A sinking feeling filled my chest. A badly injured Stephen was here, but where was Sam?

"Where has Stephen been?" I asked. "He's been somewhere in the park, unless someone drove him in and dumped him here."

"Neither the ranger nor I have seen any signs of foul play in the common areas of the park. The sheriff has had a unit at the entry all day," Snyder said. "That road's the only way in or out of the park. I'd venture to say that no one brought Stephen into the park since Standingbear set that checkpoint up this morning. Maybe I need to get that K-9 SAR team back out here."

"I think so." I watched him walk to his truck and drive off behind the ambulance, his lights flashing.

I locked the cabin door and dropped to the floor in front of it, my arms encircling Queenie. She whined as I leaned against her, holding her tight.

What had happened to Stephen? Where was Sam? The unknown ate at my heart and my mind. This was not like Sam. Our relationship was bigger than this, better than this. How could he leave me in the dark, worried and afraid? My throat closed and my eyes stung.

I clenched my fists. I didn't like this Sam, the one who had willingly disappeared into the night without a word, the one who had left me here alone, on a trip that was supposed to have been a new start to a 'together at last' relationship.

I pulled myself up and stood at the picture window in the living room, staring out at the yard and the forest beyond. Gray clouds piled up to the west, and as I watched, a bolt of lightning sliced the sky. Sam was out there somewhere, but he wasn't communicating with me.

My mind filled with possibilities. Maybe, when he'd heard about the gangsters' loot, he'd decided to double-cross Stephen and disappear with it. I laughed and sobbed at the same time. That was not Sam. He would never . . .

But I had never imagined he would leave me here alone like this, either.

My head spun. What did I really know about Sam? We had known each other as children, been playmates during my summer visits to Aunt Elizabeth in Pawhuska. Then our lives had taken different paths. He had gone to college and then law school, married Reba, and become a widower. Last spring, we had met again. Since then, hardly a day had passed that we didn't speak on the phone to touch base.

But I didn't know him. Sam had secrets, too.

The old love song Aiden had been whistling popped up in my head: *Once I had a secret love . . .* It was a sweet tune, but there was nothing secret about the love Sam and I shared. And he was correct: a more appropriate song for our love was The Fine Young Cannibals' hit from the early '90s, "She Drives Me Crazy." I loved Sam.

My heart decided to join this fight.

You know Sam's heart. You know he loves you. Every action, every word since last spring has shouted how strongly he feels for you. Don't let your fear confuse what your heart knows to be true.

I stiffened. If that was true, something had gone terribly wrong while he and Stephen were together. He was out there somewhere, alone. And possibly as injured as Stephen.

"Where is he, Queenie? Where is Sam?"

I drug myself across the room to collapse on the sofa. Queenie curled at my feet. Outside the window, the tops of the trees whipped in the wind and gray clouds piled one on top of another. I closed my eyes tightly.

"Jamie."

Sam's voice jarred me, but when I opened my eyes, the room was empty. I was still in the cabin, with its plainly decorated living room, red concrete floor, and stone fireplace.

I ran my fingers through my hair and stood. Queenie followed as I moved toward the kitchen to retrieve my phone. I had to call Cindy.

"Cindy? Are you all right?" I asked when she answered the phone.

"I'm okay. I still haven't heard from Stephen," she said in a worried voice.

"That's why I'm calling. He came here. He was injured, so I called an ambulance and they've taken him to Bartlesville."

"Oh, my God. What's wrong with him?"

"I don't know, but he's in good hands. Can you go to the hospital?"

"I can take the kids to my sister's, or she can meet me there. What happened? Was Sam with Stephen?"

"No. And Stephen was unable to tell me anything about Sam. But he made it here to my cabin—and I believe he's been in the park the whole time."

"Sam's in the park then, too. Did you check Bridget's hut?"

"It's off limits because of her death."

"Check there. Stephen might have been trying to recover something . . . incriminating." Her voice dropped to a whisper. "Maybe Sam is there. Go, Jamie. Now." She disconnected.

Something incriminating at Bridget's hut? I'd been there once and had found only her personal effects. Was there something hidden among the books on her shelves? During my previous visit, I had not checked anything too closely. I had been too aware that the site was off limits and been afraid of either being found or leaving evidence I had been there.

Bridget's hut. Cindy's voice repeated in my head. Was that where Stephen had been injured? I imagined him crawling all the way here from the shack in the woods. Was that possible?

I hurriedly brushed my hair back into a ponytail and rushed through the cabin. At the front door, I stopped. I was forgetting something, and even though I did not believe anything unexpected would happen at the hut, I knew better than to rush out unprepared. I returned to the bedroom to strap on my fanny pack and tuck my phone inside it. I pulled on a slicker and locked the cabin behind me.

Queenie and I jogged across the wide lawn, then skirted the edge of the trees until I was back at cabin seven and could step onto the trail I had taken with Queenie two days earlier.

Shadows clung to the trunks of the giant old oaks. I followed the trail, pounding along on a mix of sand and gravel until I reached a fork in the path. To the left, on the cliff trail, I had encountered Celeste and Doug Moyer. The trail to the right would soon meet the deer trail Queenie had taken to Bridget's hut.

Queenie whined. She had lost interest in the scents that usually tempted her every step of the way. Instead, she sniffed the air and turned, as if she couldn't believe what she was smelling. Today, with heavy clouds, very little light reached the forest's interior.

I kept my eyes down, watching for the deer trail that intersected the walking path. Birds called and a woodpecker drummed high above. Something squeaked underfoot, and undergrowth rustled as I disturbed an animal's search for lunch. The faint scent of skunk hung in the air.

I was certain I had walked too far and missed the intersection of the paths. I backtracked but still couldn't find the tiny trail. I turned around again, surveying my surroundings, watching for the cluster of sumac bushes Queenie and I had navigated through. I moved down the trail again, walking slowly, listening and watching. A squirrel chattered at me from the yoke of a tree.

This time, I found the path when I recognized the shimmery green sumacs clustered some twenty yards from the hiking trail. I stepped off into the brush, pulling Queenie with me, and followed the narrow, nearly hidden trail into the deeper shadows.

My first visit here, I had stumbled upon the hut unprepared. Time had been irrelevant, and the hut had seemed far from the trail junction. This time, I moved quickly, pushing through sumac, small trees, and grass. The hut appeared sooner than I expected.

I circled the structure. The door hung open. I scanned the shadows beneath the surrounding trees before stepping toward the low doorway.

"Hello? Sam? Anyone here?" The hair rose on the back of my neck. Queenie growled.

A bird chirped and a mosquito landed on my cheek. I brushed it away, then swatted around my head as I moved through a swarm of gnats hanging in the humid pre-storm air. At the hut's door, I stopped again and called out. "Sam?"

I stepped into the hut. Queenie hesitated, but followed.

Slowly, my eyes adjusted to the dimness. I could make out something on top of the bed. A pile of clothes? A person?

"Sam?"

In three bounds, I was across the little room and at the bed, reaching for the hump of blankets and expecting to feel flesh and bones beneath them. The door swung closed, throwing the room into deep shadow.

"Sam?" I reached for whoever lay on the bed, my heart sounding in my ears. My hands clutched only blankets. I searched through them, pulling the various cloths apart, and then sank into the soft mattress. He wasn't here. No one was here.

Dim light seeped in around the edges of the curtains on the windows and the skylight.

The room looked as it had during my first visit: nothing out of place other than the pile of blankets on the bed. An insect buzzed past my ear. I waved it away. Another insect buzzed past, and then another.

Bees.

Their buzzing filled the room. One landed on my hair, another on my sleeve, still another on my leg. I brushed one off my face. Swatting at them would anger them further, and they were angry enough. Dozens of them zoomed around the tiny cabin, and it seemed there were more of them flying in every second.

Where were they coming from?

Something pinched my cheek, and immediately, the site of the pinch began to throb. I remembered that when stung by a bee, you should not pull the stinger out or more venom will pump into the site of the sting. I had no choice but to tolerate the painful sting and make every effort to calm both the bees and me.

I leaped across the room to the door and pushed, bees buzzing all around me, landing on my ears, my face, and my hair. Queenie and I had to get out.

I threw my weight against the door, expecting to fall out into the woods. Instead, the door didn't budge. I shoved again, then grabbed the latch and shook it.

We were locked in.

CHAPTER 29

I pounded on the door and shook the handle. Bees buzzed in my ears. Others landed on my face, my hair, my sleeves. The insects swarmed around me in the tiny hut, buzzing angrily. Their only way out—and ours—was blocked. I dove for the bed, covered myself with a blanket, and pitched another over Queenie on the floor. Something sharp pricked my hand: another bee sting.

What if I had developed a bee allergy, like Bridget? How long before my throat began to swell and my air passages narrowed? My breathing quickened and my heart raced.

Someone had blocked the door from the outside, leaving me inside with an angry swarm of honeybees. Who would have done that? And why?

Another bee stung the back of my neck. I shook out one of the quilts and wrapped myself in it, leaving only my face exposed, so I could peer around the dim interior of the hut.

Bridget's beekeeping garb was inside the trunk.

With the quilt wrapped around me for protection, I reached for the trunk and pulled the lid open. The white equipment shone clearly in the dim lighting. I shoved the quilt away, flicked my hair to remove any bees that might be entangled there, and slipped the veiled hat over my head.

Bees landed on my arms. They were unable to sting me through my clothing, but my hands were a different story. I dug in the trunk for Bridget's bee gloves and slipped them on after gently brushing the tops of my hands on the edge of the bed to remove any bees. The swollen sting on the back of my hand throbbed.

On the floor, under the blanket, Queenie whined.

With the netted hat and the gloves protecting my most exposed and crucial body parts, I began to calm down, and as I did, fewer bees seemed to buzz around me. I remembered what Celeste had said. The bees 'liked' Bridget. She wasn't afraid of them. She 'talked' to the bees.

I breathed deeply several times and said, "It's all right. Everything is all right."

The bees didn't listen.

"It's all right. Everything is all right," I repeated. And repeated again.

I searched for the bees' entry point. As small as the hut was, it didn't take long to find. I'd seen something similar at a nature center's bee exhibit: plastic tubing had been inserted into the casing where the stovepipe met the top of the slanted roofline. Someone had placed a container of bees high up on the outside wall, with their only possible exit through the tube and into the hut.

The bees, Queenie, and I were trapped.

Two bees landed on the net of my headgear, buzzing, angry. One glance at the sleeves of my slicker revealed a dozen bees crawling; one tried over and over to sting through the thick waterproof material.

"Everything's okay, guys. Let's not be upset." Were the bees listening to me? Would they crawl through the gaps in my clothing?

I banged once again at the door, shaking it. The boards creaked, but neither the hinges nor the latch gave way. My activity upset the bees: their buzzing increased in volume. They buzzed about my head, and I could imagine dozens of them crawling on my back. Hundreds swarmed throughout the small room, covering every available surface.

"Hey, now. Let's calm down. I'm not going to hurt you, and

there's no honey in here for me to steal, is there? This isn't your hive." I pulled in a deep breath and then let it out slowly. A bee landed on the net in front of my eyes.

On the floor, Queenie whined. Were the bees stinging the dog? If so, would she have a reaction? I had to get both of us out, fast.

On my first visit to the hut, I had seen a bee smoker at the bottom of Bridget's trunk. I jerked the lid open again and dug for the odd contraption. What had I once read about how to get it working? Fuel for the smoker had to be lit on fire and then inserted. Pumping the bellows on the smoker released the smoke into the air. Where was the fuel?

Once again, I dug through the trunk. In a box in the bottom of the trunk, I found a box of matches and a bag of thick papery discs. It seemed like a likely fuel, one that would be easy to burn. I could stuff one into the smoker and light it with a match. The question was, in this confined space, with no certain way out, should I light it?

Somewhere in the back of my mind, I remembered reading that a smoker was for use near a hive or in an apiary, when bees were disturbed and afraid, alert to intruders. It calmed them and sent them back to their various assigned hive duties. We weren't in a hive. There were no duties for them to perform except to sting whatever alien creature had disrupted their world.

Would the smoke send the bees into a stinging frenzy? That was the last thing I wanted. I put the smoker, fuel and matches back in the trunk.

I thought about bees. Even though bees are insects, they are intelligent ones. They live in a highly structured society, and communicate with one another. They can sense fear.

In this situation, what would Bridget, or Stephen do? I sat down on the bed.

Looking down, I worried more about Queenie. The dog huddled at my feet, peeking out from under the blanket. "You're okay. Everything's all right. I promise, it really is."

The volume of the bee's buzzing dropped. "You're okay, I'm okay. We're all okay. Let's just calm down."

I repeated the words again, and then again. Slowly, the buzzing quieted and the insects began to drop to the floor, the surface of the table, or the bed. They dropped from my sleeves and from the netting of my helmet. A low humming pervaded the room as the bees stopped flying and huddled on the lower surfaces.

I unzipped my fanny pack and pulled out my phone. The screen lit up, but nothing happened when I tried to make a call. I was out of range of the nearest tower. At my feet, Queenie whined.

I rattled the door once more, my mind spinning in angry circles.

Who had locked me in?

That brought to mind another question: who would be comfortable enough with bees to have brought them here and set up this trap, including creating a passage for them to crawl into the hut?

Only one person came to mind. And that person was now in the Bartlesville hospital. Was there someone else in the park who knew bees?

"It's all right. Everyone's okay, see? Everybody stay calm." My voice quivered. I wasn't fooling myself, was I fooling the bees?

Queenie whined. She lunged for one corner of the back wall, then scratched at it. I needed more light to get a better look at whatever the dog was interested in. I pulled the curtain off a side window. A few bees flew up from the bed and headed lazily for the light. I stepped back from the window and turned to the corner of the hut. More bees rose up from the floor and buzzed toward the window.

"See, everything's fine. I'm okay, you're okay."

I leaned over Queenie to see the back wall. The rear section of the hut was different. The vertical wall planks had a slice through them about two feet up; a loop made from a leather cord hung down from about halfway across the slice. I pulled the loop and the wall section moved. I tugged harder and the section came loose and fell into the hut, leaving a dark opening.

Bridget had built an escape hatch.

Of course she had. If she was hiding, as Celeste had said, she would need to have more than one way to get out of her hut should the need arise.

I stooped lower. The opening went down into the ground and turned. A tunnel.

I reached into my fanny pack again. Inside were my trusty flashlight and a few emergency-type tools, matches, and a magnifying glass. I flicked on the flashlight.

"Here we go, Queenie." I ignored the pounding of my heart and the lump in my throat. I should be getting used to crawling through tunnels now. Tunnels had become a part of my life—both in my nightmares and in real life. But if I wanted out of the hut to save Queenie and myself—and to find Sam—I had to take Bridget's emergency exit.

I knelt and shone the light into the blackness. No spider webs. I pulled off the netted helmet and laid it on the bed. Holding the small flashlight in my mouth, I crawled into the tunnel, grateful for the long, thick beekeeper's gloves that protected my hands and elbows from the hard, rocky earth.

The light revealed planks placed every few feet or so on both sidewalls of the tunnel, supporting horizontal ceiling braces.

Queenie whined behind me. My heart pounded in my throat.

"Come on, girl." I crawled forward on my hands and knees. Stones bit into my bony knees through the fabric of my jeans. Queenie's nails scratched on the tunnel floor behind me as we moved forward.

My flashlight soon revealed the end of the tunnel, a square panel only a few feet further. I crawled up to it and stopped. When I shoved against the wood panel, it flipped upward. Dirt rained down. I scooted beneath it and crawled out onto the mossy forest floor. Queenie pulled herself out behind me and lay panting on the moist earth. The wooden panel dropped back into place behind us, perfectly camouflaged by a coating of moss.

Thank God, thank God, thank God. I brushed myself off and stood, then turned in a circle to view my surroundings and slow my heart. I brushed leaves across the angled opening and then pulled off the gloves and tucked them under a bush.

The tunnel had brought us out into the forest only three or four yards behind Bridget's hut; I could make out her back wall, hidden in the vines and low understory growth. The ground had eroded into a gully with sides covered by ground-creeping vines, pebbles, and dirt.

Queenie growled. The ridge of hair on her back rose up and her tail lifted to point. I listened, still not hearing what the dog heard. A crow squawked above us and insects trilled in the grass at the base of a nearby tree. Something small rustled in the leaves. A vole or mouse?

Then, not far away, a male voice cried out. "Help me! Somebody, please! Help!"

CHAPTER 30

I followed Queenie as she forced her way through the vines and underbrush in the direction of the voice. My arms and legs trembled, and my heart pounded. Was it Sam? Where was he?

The voice cried out again, sounding even more desperate. "Somebody, please."

We crashed through an opening in the foliage and onto a well-worn animal trail. Queenie stopped to investigate under a bush, now unconcerned about the voice we'd heard calling. I listened to the man cry out again. Between Queenie's lack of concern and the low timbre of the voice, I knew that whoever was calling for help was not Sam.

"Help me! Is anybody there?"

I pushed on down the path and then veered through the trees, avoiding the densest undergrowth of thorny vines and brambles, keeping Queenie's leash short and tight. The man groaned.

Bernard Wood lay on the ground, one leg bent at an awkward angle, his white face contorted in pain. He grabbed at his foot with gloved hands as tears streamed down his face.

"Oh, God, somebody please help me!"

The toothed jaws of a rusted animal trap had snapped closed around Bernie's ankle; dark smears of blood coated his lower pant leg and foot.

A hundred thoughts raced through my mind as I rushed the last few feet to reach the anguished man.

Had Bernie set up the bees so that they swarmed into Bridget's hut? Otherwise, what was Bernie doing out here off the path, where we'd all been warned not to go?

The steel contraption clamped on his ankle was not the kind of trap I had expected the Wildlife Department to set. This trap was designed to maim, not to catch an animal for transport and release elsewhere in the wild.

Even more disconcerting, this trap had been set not far from Bridget's hut.

A growl rumbled in Queenie's throat as I dropped to the ground next to Bernie's feet.

"Jamie! Thank God." Bernie's eyes closed and popped open again. "I stepped in one of the damn cougar traps. Can you give me a hand?" A rivulet of sweat ran down his dirt-smeared face as he reached toward me. Bernie's eyes were wide and dark. He clawed at his foot. "It hurts terribly. Can't you do something?"

The teeth of the trap bit into his left ankle. A thick, rusty chain attached to the trap ran across the ground to a peg hammered deep into the trunk of a nearby elm tree.

I stayed out of reach of the big man's grasping hands as I squatted a few feet away and studied his foot. I moved closer, then grabbed each side of the trap and tried to pull, but the strength in my arms was no match for the trap's spring.

"I'll have to go for help. No way can I pull this open myself."

"Please, don't leave me alone again. I'm going to pass out from the pain. And the cougar. Oh, God. I'm dinner just waiting to be served."

I peeked over my shoulder at ancient oaks and elms then looked down at the older man. My heart was a stone inside my chest. A few days ago, I had liked this man and his wife. Not now.

"Did you lock me into Bridget's hut, Bernie?" I asked, eying his gloves.

His eyes rolled in his head, the sclera showing all around his pupils. "I don't have anything against you. Help me! Please!"

"You closed me in there? With the bees?" I inched farther away. His hands reached for me. "Why, Bernie?"

His face contorted. "It's Betty. She hates you," he groaned. He pinched his eyes shut and tears leaked from them to run down his sweaty face.

"Why?"

"She hated your mother, and once she found out who you were . . ." He gasped and reached for his foot again. "Ow! Please do something!"

Queenie yipped. She gazed up at me, drool stringing down from her jowls.

"Why did she hate my mother?"

"Oh, God, can't you help me?" Bernie gritted his teeth. "I was thinking coming here would take us back to our youth, make us feel young again. I shouldn't have brought her here. Even after fifty years, her memories of that summer's church camp are too painful. I didn't know she knew Bridget lived out here, or that she'd been taunting her, sending hateful anonymous notes for years. Owww. Jamie, please."

This man had locked me in a small, closed-in space with a hive of bees because his wife hated my mother? Not only was that ridiculous, it was unbelievable. There had to be more to this vendetta than he was saying.

Did they know about the gangsters' loot, too, and Stephen's search for it?

If Bernard had been willing to trap me in the hut with the bees, what might he have done to Sam and Stephen? Was Bernard responsible for Stephen's injuries? And even more importantly, did he know where Sam was?

"Where's Betty? Where's Sam?" I stood at the helpless man's feet, my heart pounding in my ears.

"Oh, God, Jamie. Please, get this trap off my foot. I promise, if you will, I'll help you save Sam. If we delay, I can't help you save him. He could end up on the rocks below the overlook, like Patrick Gallagher."

I charged through the trees, tugging a reluctant Queenie behind me. We crashed through the undergrowth.

Bernie Wood screamed after us. "Jamie! I need help! I'm going to die! Jamie? Jamie!"

Vines caught at my face, my hair, my clothes. Queenie and I plowed through the dense foliage and back onto the nature path. After a few yards, the path forked. My blood pumped adrenaline through my body. We ran.

Don't let me be too late!

I leaped over roots on the worn trail, and every few yards I lifted Queenie over downed tree limbs. Finally, the trees began to thin; bits of gray sky poked through the thick web of branches overhead. Queenie's breath came in ragged gasps, loud and labored as she struggled to keep up with me on her short basset hound legs.

The landscape opened to the lawn surrounding the group camp. The overlook was straight ahead. I pounded across the cement sidewalk and around the building onto the flagstones, then rushed up to the ledge and peered over. Far below, on the rocky bank beside the rushing river, lay a broken body. Black hair floated in the moving water.

I couldn't breathe. If it was Sam . . . Was it Sam? I managed to pull enough air into my lungs to scream. "Sam!"

Footsteps thundered on the flagstones behind me. A light rain began to patter down.

"Jamie, step back." Doug Moyer grabbed my shoulders.

I tried to twist away as I looked for a way down the perilous cliff.

"Jamie, no." Moyer kept a tight hold on my arm. "There's no way down from here. We sent a crew after we got the call; they're making their way down from farther upstream. We'll know soon enough who it is."

"Have you seen Betty Wood?" I asked. I wasn't sure if he could hear me over the pounding of my heart. "She did this."

Doug loosened his grip on my arm. "Betty Wood? Did what?"

"Bernie told me she did. Bernie–"

"Bernie? I'm not following you. They are headed home to Wichita." He shook his head and frowned.

"Don't let them leave. Betty and Bernie . . . I think they hurt Stephen. I think they've hurt Sam. And Bernie's caught in an animal trap by Bridget's place."

"What?" Doug pulled out his radio. "The Wildlife Department crew didn't set any traps near there."

"Well, he's in a trap, bleeding."

I was vaguely aware that life was happening around me. Minutes were ticking past. The rain was dripping. Birds were squawking from the trees. But the world was fuzzy, and in the center of my vision, all I could see was the broken body far below at the edge of the water.

Voices shouted. Doug grabbed my arm again as the two of us looked down at the police team wading into the stream.

Bile rose in my throat; I pulled away from Doug and threw up. My head swam.

Doug turned a dial on his handheld radio and spoke again. "Can you get an ID?"

My hands lifted involuntarily. I didn't want to know whose body lay below on the rocks, and yet I had to know.

A roar filled my ears; my hands shook.

On the flagstone next to me, Queenie lay on her side, her thick short legs stretched away from her body, her tongue lolling on the rock beneath her, leaving a splotch of wet bigger than the marks left by the light rain.

Another voice sounded clear in the moisture-drenched nearly-summer air. "It's Betty Wood."

I sank against the wall and down to the ground next to Queenie.

Betty. It was Betty. *Not Sam.*

My breath whooshed from my body. I rested my head against my knees, my arms wrapped around them. Betty lay far below. It was Betty who had fallen from the overlook.

Where was Sam? A terrible thought occurred to me. Had Bernie killed Sam and Betty before locking me in Bridget's hut? It made no sense, but I had no other idea as to who might be behind recent events. Bernie had already shown himself to be a liar. There was no trusting anything he said. I wasn't sure Aiden was much better.

Doug fiddled with his radio's dial. "Celeste? I need your help."

CHAPTER 31

As I waited for Celeste, tension gradually released its paralyzing grip on my muscles. In the creek, the deputies loaded Betty onto a gurney. The soft shower of rain kept falling.

Thank God it wasn't Sam.

The recovery team began the long trek back up the creek to the spot where they had accessed the water. I watched them pick their way among the rocks, slipping on the mossy places and searching for new footholds against the rushing water.

I thought of Bernie in the trap. Had anyone found him yet? I had not heard Doug give an alert over his radio about sending help to the injured man.

Queenie sat at my feet, watching with big brown eyes, her long, stiff tail tucked against her body. A twinge of guilt nipped at my brain. Poor Bernie had been in great pain. And I had left him alone.

He deserved it.

Not far away, a car door slammed; seconds later, Celeste rushed up and grabbed Doug's arm. "Betty Wood? I can't believe it."

Doug looked down at her. His hard look softened and his eyes lit up. He glanced at me and stiffened again. "Jamie found Bernard in the woods, caught in a cougar trap."

"What?"

I was certain the trap Bernie had stumbled into was not a

sanctioned cougar trap set by the Oklahoma Department of Wildlife Conservation.

"Is help on its way to Bernie?" I interrupted the couple, who had turned their backs to me and were speaking to one another in low tones.

"Not yet," Doug responded over his shoulder. "We don't have enough men on the ground." He and Celeste moved closer. "The maintenance crew is headed there now to pry that trap open, and I am sure Karen has notified the sheriff and called an ambulance."

Celeste adjusted the hood of her slicker as she peered at my face. "You look exhausted. And your cheek is swollen. Did something sting you?" She patted my arm. "Come with me. I'll take you back to your cabin."

I pulled on the leash and Queenie followed us across the flagstones to Celeste's small white truck. I lifted Queenie into the cab and climbed in after her, closed the door, and rested my head against the window. My bones ached; my legs and arms were heavy and useless. The bee stings on my hand, neck and face throbbed. I studied the one swollen, red bump I could see.

"What happened to your hand and your face?" Celeste asked as she flipped on the windshield wipers and steered the truck onto the asphalt road leading away from the group camp.

"Bee stings."

"Where were you? Have you been at the apiary?" Her voice rose a notch. "I stay away from bees, even though Bridget tried to convince me they were harmless. So did Doug. What kind of naturalist am I anyway if I can't even handle a little ol' bee buzzing around?" She snickered. "Truth is I just can't handle insects, period."

I turned my forehead against the cool glass of the window. The world began a slow spin. Queenie woofed and placed one huge paw on my thigh.

"So, still no Sam," Celeste said. "I heard his cousin surfaced and went to the hospital. You have got to be worried."

Worried? What an understatement. I blinked in an attempt to settle the wavering wall of green outside the truck window.

"I thought Sam would be back by now." Celeste sighed. "You've still no idea where he might have gone?"

"I believe he was with his cousin. But now his cousin is in the hospital, unconscious." I pictured that body, far below on the rocky bank of the stream. It could have been Sam. "And I'm surprised about Betty."

The truck rumbled down the road. I pressed my throbbing cheek against the window glass.

"Me, too," Celeste said. "She was always so jolly. It had to have been an accident."

The image of Betty lying far below the overlook, her dark hair swirling in the muddy water, superimposed itself over my memory of her scarfing down half a hamburger on our cabin patio Saturday night.

"And you found Bernie caught in that animal trap." Celeste sighed as she turned the truck into the cabin area. "Bridget always said it would catch someone unawares. I told her it was dangerous."

"Bridget set that awful old trap? Why? Didn't she know it was dangerous?" I recalled the huge rusty, jagged teeth of the tight trap. It was likely that Bernie's ankle was broken. His recovery from that wound would take time as well as a tetanus shot.

"She set it a few weeks ago. Told me she needed an alarm system. I think she would have booby-trapped the entire perimeter of her hut if she could have, and she did have a few cans and kitchen utensils hung in bushes nearby to make noise if someone snuck up on her." Celeste pulled into the driveway of cabin two and pulled the truck's parking brake. "When I convinced her those items were a dead giveaway to the location of her hut, she took them down."

"Was she frightened of someone specific or just concerned

about prowlers?" Bernie had told me Betty had been taunting Bridget; she'd probably sent the creepy jump rope rhyme. Was the rhyme the reason Bridget had booby-trapped the area? "Any idea what happened a few weeks ago?"

Celeste shrugged. "I've thought about that. I saw Bridget arguing with Aiden once after he came to research the book. Later, when I asked her about it, she pretended they had only been talking. As I think back, it was soon after that when she set the trap."

"Did she have anything of value someone might want to take?" I searched my memory of the well-stocked cabin. Food, books, soap, candles, and everyday goods.

Celeste shook her head. "I think she was afraid of being found."

"By whom?" Why would she have been frightened of Betty? Why had Betty terrorized her? There was more to this story than I knew.

"I don't know. The only name she ever mentioned was that of her friend–Mary."

My mother.

I lingered in the doorway, watching Celeste drive away, then closed and locked the door to the cabin. I hadn't invited her in. I didn't have any polite conversation left in me. In the little bathroom, I treated throbbing bee stings on my face, neck, and hands.

Stephen was in critical condition and Sam was still missing. Bridget had set an animal trap for protection, and died from a head wound while hiding in a tree. The only name she'd ever mentioned from her past was 'Mary.' The bits and pieces of what I knew about Bridget didn't add up to much.

There was no telepathy between my mother and me. We had never had one of those relationships where we would say, when the other person called on the phone, 'I was thinking about you.' I blamed it on my mom's unwillingness to let her guard down and truly connect with me, either mentally or physically.

I pulled my cell phone out of my pack and set it on the table. I had to give it one more try.

My phone rang. *Sam?* My heart fluttered with hope.

The caller ID read 'Mom.' Surprise was not a large enough word for the feeling that overcame me.

"Mother," I breathed, trying to keep the quiver out of my voice.

"Jamie? Do you have time to talk?" She sounded breathless, too, but with urgency rather than hope—or its opposite, despair.

I dropped onto the sofa. Unbelievable. My mother on the other end of the phone, asking if I had time to talk? Usually, she launched into whatever topic had provoked the call, or a complaint.

"I'm at the cabin. No one here but me."

I imagined her in her Rio Rancho home, sipping tea and staring out the window at Sandia Mountain across town, beyond the sea of New Mexican tile rooftops. Something was different today; there was a hesitancy in her voice I wasn't used to hearing.

"Jamie, it's all this talk of the past. I don't want to think about it. But I can't stop now that you've started it all."

"Mom, it's taken over my life. Sam is missing and his cousin Stephen is badly injured."

"Oh, no. I didn't want . . . I didn't think . . . Jamie . . ." her voice faded.

What were the chances my mother knew enough to end this whole thing? Did she know some secret about Bridget that could explain what had happened and tell me where Sam was?

"Mom, if you'll talk to me about that summer and what happened with Patrick Gallagher . . ." I closed my eyes and ran my fingertips over my forehead. "I want Sam here with me, Mom. I'm not sure I'll ever see him again." I clenched my fist.

"Oh, Jamie. Surely things aren't that dire."

"Today, Bernie Wood told me that his wife, Betty, was going to push Sam over the wall at the overlook, but when I got there, it was Betty lying far below. It could have been Sam, Mother. Maybe it was supposed to have been Sam. I want him back. I need to know it all, Mother. Please tell me everything."

"Bernie? Betty? They're both there?" She gulped. "That's not possible."

"They *were* both here. Now Betty's dead. You knew Aiden, too, didn't you?"

"Aiden?" Her voice shook. "Poor Aiden."

"Mother, why are all of these people you knew here at the park now?"

"Oh, Jamie. I wish I could make it all go away." Her voice broke. "Was it all my fault?"

I sensed that she wasn't asking the question of me, but of herself—this was not the proper, confident, and aloof woman who had raised me.

"Mother?" I wanted her to tell it straight for once in her life, not to beat around the bush and keep half of whatever-it-was secret. "I need to hear it all from you, from the beginning. I won't judge you. Whatever it is you don't want to admit could be the very thing to help me find Sam. Maybe save his life. This is life-or-death serious."

"It was life-or-death serious all those years ago, and we were too young and naïve to see it."

Resolve strengthened her voice. I sensed that whatever my mother told me next would be the truth.

"Jamie, what I told you before about all of us horsing around on the ledge was not exactly true. We were horsing around, but it wasn't light-hearted. There was teasing—even bullying."

"Was Aiden there?"

"Not that night. But he was at the camp, another counselor. Aiden was . . . I want to be clear about this. I'm neither condoning nor judging what he was—or is—it wasn't something we talked about. I could hardly imagine such a thing was possible in my sheltered upbringing."

"What are you talking about?" I pulled my feet up under me and spread the afghan across my lap.

"I mean, for someone of one sex to love—physically—someone of the same sex. And for them both to desire each other." Her voice shook.

"Aiden? Are you telling me he's a homosexual?"

"Yes. Or he was then."

"I don't think being a homosexual is something you can change at will, Mother, not even over time. Aiden is an intelligent man and an expert on the WPA and the CCC. He's here researching a book he's writing. How does his sexuality relate to what happened?"

"Bernie and Betty Wood have seen him?"

"Yes. They attended a program he gave at the group camp Sunday night."

"Did Bernie heckle him?"

I remembered the odd interruption to Aiden's talk, and how Bernie and Betty had left the hall before the program was finished. "How did you know?"

"He always bullied Aiden. Bernie loved girls, you know. Any girl. It was hard for him to tolerate a man who didn't. Plus, Aiden was so into the history of the place."

"He was interested in the CCC camp ruins even back then?"

"Yes. His father had worked at the camp. So had Bernie's. The two men knew one another, I think."

"And Patrick Gallagher's father worked at the camp, too, didn't he?"

She pulled in a breath. "Yes. And that's when it all began."

"But the CCC camp was in ruins long before the summer you worked there." I rubbed at my temples, but my mind wasn't clicking. How did all of this tie in to Bridget or to Sam's disappearance, not to mention the apiary and gangsters' loot?

"You haven't fit the pieces together." Mother cleared her throat. "I can help."

"Please."

"During the 1930s, the young men were working in the park, building walls and park structures, even cabins. Some of them uncovered an old hideout, barely inside the park's property lines, probably once used by gangsters—or certainly by moonshiners."

I thought of the old wall, where we had found mother's name linked with Patrick's. The ruins of the old hideout?

"These CCC men were gathering bricks and other building materials for the park structures. Some of them pulled bricks and stone from the ruins of that old cabin. And a couple of them found something beneath a wall they were dismantling. They dug it up." Mother paused. I could hear her swallow as she drank something. She cleared her throat. "When the construction of park facilities was completed at one place, some of the men moved on to other projects. Some of them found construction work in the same area. The Depression ended with the start of World War II, and the camp closed."

"What did they dig up? Was it the gangsters' stash? Explain."

"I'm getting there, Jamie Lynn. Listen."

"Okay. I'm listening." I scratched Queenie behind the ears.

"Twenty years passed. Now, it's the summer of 1955, and all of us are counselors in the park. The guys knew their fathers had worked together at the camp. They'd all heard talk of the loot, but no one had told them what happened to it, only the story of its discovery and the known fact that one of the men—no one knew which one—had hidden it and not told the others." She coughed. "Each man suspected the other two. They became enemies. So the three boys got it into their heads that the money, much of it in Peace Silver Dollars, must still be there. None of the three had seen evidence of money for luxuries when they were growing up. Every spare minute at camp, the boys were scouring the park, searching for the treasure their fathers had spoken about. But they didn't know for certain where the original hideout was located."

"Did they find the treasure or the old hideout?" I asked, scooting forward to the edge of the sofa. Doug Moyer had shown us a Peace Silver Dollar on Saturday night during his 'ghost' program. Not all of what he had told us had been made up.

"One night, Patrick, Bridget, and I were out roaming around, talking about the gangsters' loot and all the old stories. We wandered up to the old CCC camp, and in the meadow west of there, we found a grouping of rocks. One of the rocks had been carved with an odd symbol, two wavy lines like the Native American symbol for water. Patrick wondered if the symbol meant something, if maybe something was buried under the rock, or somewhere near. So we dug around the rock. We found an old metal box with a rusty padlock."

I realized I was holding my breath and gently released it. "What was in the box? The Peace Dollars?"

"Patrick wanted Aiden to see the box before we opened it, and he didn't want Bernie to get wind that we had found it. We had to find another place to put it." Mother's voice dropped low. "We buried it again, in an out-of-the-way place where we didn't think the others would find it. Patrick, Bridget, and I buried it. And he carved my name with his on the wall to mark the spot."

"On the old wall?"

"That wall once defined the yard around the old dugout where the outlaws hid. Bridget and I were the only ones who knew where the box was after Patrick fell from the overlook the next night. I don't even know for sure whether or not he told Aiden where it was."

"What do you think happened to Patrick that night? Did he fall, or was he pushed?"

Mother sighed. "I don't want to believe he was pushed. I want it to have been an accident. But no one knows."

"Someone knows, Mother." I chose my words carefully. "And Bridget's death was not an accident, either. She had a severe head wound. And she had climbed a tree to hide. She died there, then fell. Later that morning, the branch came down on top of her."

Mother gasped.

"Why do you think Bridget became a hermit, Mother? And who could she have been hiding from? I learned today that she and Aiden argued the day before her death. Would Aiden have killed her?"

"Oh, my. I can't imagine Aiden doing such a thing. He was always so gentle. But as far as the treasure, she probably dug up the money at some point. You said she's been living out there alone all these years. How did she buy supplies? What did she eat? She had to have used the money from the strong-box."

"According to the park naturalist, Celeste, Bridget was self-sufficient. Grew vegetables, made soap and candles." I rubbed the back of my neck. My feet tingled.

"But there's something else, Jamie. If I'm going to tell it, I have to tell it all. I don't want to cover anything up or have you misunderstand."

"I'm listening."

"You know the inscription you found on the wall? It didn't mean what you think. Patrick didn't love me. I was his 'girl-friend' to throw off suspicion. He and Aiden were . . . together." Her voice cracked on the last word.

Together? Pain dripped from my mother's words. She *had* loved him.

"Who else knew?"

"I didn't think anyone else knew. But when they found him at the bottom of the cliff, my first thought was that someone else found out their secret and killed him because of who he was and who he loved. Someone like Bernie."

I hung up the phone a few minutes later.

Bernie. Betty. Aiden. Patrick Gallagher. Bridget. My mother, Mary Jamison. Their names circled around in my head.

Queenie whined. I poured some kibble into her bowl. Where did Stephen and Sam fit into this now? Did Bridget tell

Stephen where the remainder of the loot was, like Cindy had said?

I punched in the number for the park office on my cell phone. Karen picked up.

"Can you have Ranger Doug Moyer call me, please? It's Jamie Aldrich, and it's urgent," I blurted.

"Actually, I see his truck pulling up outside the office. Should I have him come to your cabin?"

"That would be great. Cabin two. I'll be waiting outside." I grabbed Queenie's leash and the two of us waited on the small porch for Doug Moyer.

CHAPTER 32

I picked Queenie up and raced for Moyer's truck, jerked the door open, and hopped up into the cab before the vehicle had pulled to a complete stop.

"We need to go back to the old ruins, where Sam and I were when we met you last Saturday. Do you have a shovel?"

The ranger gestured toward the back end of the truck as he backed out of the driveway, putting the truck in gear before I had time to buckle my seat belt. "What's up?"

Dirt splotched his cheek and bits of leaves were stuck to his pants. Had he been in the forest again with Celeste, grabbing a passionate moment? Another time, I might have quizzed him about it, but not now, not when I was close to figuring out this puzzle and, hopefully, to finding Sam.

"Sam and I didn't tell you what we found before the limb fell that morning," I said as I settled Queenie on my lap. "In all the excitement of finding Bridget's body it had been unimportant, but now I think it might be the key to all of this."

"A key? To Bridget's death? Even the mystery of where your fiancé went?" Moyer asked, keeping his eyes on the road ahead as he navigated onto one of the rocky, uneven service roads.

"Yes. Everything is tangled together, as unbelievable as that seems. How close can we get to the place that limb fell, near that old wall?"

"I'll use an access road to get as close as I can, but this

truck is bigger than an ATV and unable to handle the rough and narrow trails. We'll have to leave the truck and walk."

"Hurry." My heart pounded. I was certain we were about to find Sam. We had to be.

My mind worked. I knew the location where Mother and Patrick had reburied the 'money box.' Maybe Sam had told Stephen about that same wall and the Bee Water symbol on the brick. Had the two of them gone there to search?

Moyer stopped the truck when the rocky track we'd been following abruptly ended in dense vegetation. We climbed out. I knew approximately where we were but had no idea how to get to the site of the old wall from here. I lifted Queenie from the truck and snapped on her leash.

"This way," he said. The ranger headed into the trees, carrying his shovel, following a faint trail through the underbrush over freshly crushed vegetation. Were we following Sam and Stephen's tracks? Had Stephen crawled all the way from here?

Queenie and I kept close to Doug. We made our way slowly, stepping around deadfall from the previous winter as well as new bushes and trees that sprouted from the spongy, leaf-covered forest floor. Above us, light filtered in through the tree canopy; birds flitted in the upper branches. The sweet, putrid odor of something dead and the scent of honeysuckle floated together in the air as we forged through the forest.

"How far is it?" I asked.

"Not much farther. Stay close. I think there's another trap in here somewhere. Wouldn't want you to get your foot caught in one like Bernard Wood did."

"You knew Bridget had set traps?"

"Yes. I told her to get rid of them. Bridget didn't always do what she was told," Doug said as he pushed on ahead.

In my mind, I could still hear Bernie's cries for help. Most likely, he was in the hospital now. Did he know Betty had fallen from the overlook and died? I didn't want to think about

Bernie and what he had said. I didn't want any of it to be true. But, why would Bernie lie about it?

Queenie huffed along, following Doug Moyer. I was careful to step exactly where the ranger stepped. He stopped to take in the vine-covered trees and the fallen tree trunk that now blocked our path, then turned to the left and struck off again.

"Are we almost there?" I asked. I sounded like a little child riding in a car to some faraway place; I had no sense of the distance to the wall and the ruins of the old gangster hideout. When Doug stopped again, he pointed at a pile of bricks jutting up from the earth, part of an old wall.

I scanned the area. This was not the same place where Sam and I had found the inscription on the wall, but much deeper into the woods. Here, the forest floor showed signs of disturbance, as if someone had raked the leaf debris, smoothing it out over ground that had recently been disturbed. Queenie rushed to the site, a low growl in her throat. Her nose worked over the spot before she began to dig furiously at the earth.

"Queenie's found something."

Doug watched her. "You think she smells something there?"

"I'm sure of it. Queenie, stop. Queenie?"

The dog whined as her feet worked, throwing earth behind her through her legs. When she stopped and began to lick at something on the ground, I stepped closer. No telling what it was—something dead, no doubt, that smelled delicious to the dog.

"What in the . . ."

The dog licked the dirt and nosed at something.

"Queenie, drop it," I said as I leaned down, imagining a dead mouse or baby bird that had fallen from a nest in the tree above.

Something glistened in the dim light. A turquoise and coral ring gleamed on the outstretched fingers of a human hand.

Stars swirled in my head and time stopped. My future—

days of laughter and hand-holding, nights of comfort in the arms I loved—exploded in slow motion like a fireworks display and faded away.

"Oh, my God. Sam!"

CHAPTER 33

I joined Queenie in her dig, clawing at the earth with my hands, shoving dirt aside as I tried to uncover Sam. "Help me! Give me the shovel." I whirled to grab it from Doug Moyer.

Six feet away, the ranger stood grinning, leaning on the shovel. "You two seem to be doing well on your own. I'll help make the hole a little deeper after a bit. I want to see your face when you get him uncovered. There is a small chance that he's still alive. He's only been under there a couple of hours."

My heart stopped. Doug Moyer was a cold-blooded killer.

I returned to my frantic digging, shoving my fingers into the soft forest earth and scooping it away from what was now taking on the shape of a human body. Queenie growled and moaned at the same time; the same sound of anguish filled my own head.

Queenie and I pawed at the ground, moving soil and humus to the sides. I scraped the earth away from Sam's face, digging out the fine silt caked between his lips. Queenie licked his face.

"Sam? Sam can you hear me?" I grabbed his arms and pulled him up from the shallow grave. Dirt clods fell from his body. His chin dropped onto his chest. "Sam!"

I shook him gently. Beneath the coating of dirt on his face, what looked like dried blood covered the side of his head. His right eye had swollen to the size of half a baseball. Was he breathing?

"Sam," I moaned. "Please, please don't die." I leaned closer. A soft puff of air hit my cheek.

"Sam!" I shifted, pulling his body farther up and away from the hole. "Sam. Wake up." I shook him again. Could he hear me?

Doug Moyer began to whistle. A few notes in, I knew the song. 'Secret Love.'

"Shut up!" I shouted at Doug. I shook Sam gently.

Was Sam dead? Was our future ending here? Now?

"Do you know that song, Jamie? Funny thing, Aiden Blunt introduced me to it. It has sort of become my theme song. You know Celeste? We're lovers. The two of us are going to enjoy this treasure together once you tell me where it is."

I bent closer to Sam; his breath tickled my cheek. "Sam! Wake up!" I clutched him to me, heartened by the feel of his warm breath soft and shallow on my neck.

From immediately behind me, Doug Moyer whispered in my ear, "That's enough, Jamie. He's sedated; no use trying to wake him up. I'm only going to put him—and you—underground again."

I jerked my head back and connected with his chin. Moyer lost his balance and crashed into a bush, still gripping the shovel.

He stumbled to his feet and glared. "Don't give me any trouble. We can get this over real fast with a minimum of fuss. Tell me where it is."

I scraped more dirt from Sam's face.

"You know what happened to Bridget. She hid from me but died all the same. The same thing would have happened to Stephen if he hadn't managed to get away. Tell me where the strongbox is."

I patted Sam's back and then felt the steady but weak pulse in his neck.

"You two wanted to get married so you could be together forever. You may not be married, but you'll be together here until the end of time." Moyer lifted the blade of the shovel.

I rolled to the left.

The shovel sliced into the ground.

Queenie snarled and leaped through the air.

She yelped. Her body crashed into the underbrush.

I rolled to my feet.

The shovel slammed into my head.

It was raining; the hard drops smelled and tasted like dirt. They pelted my cheeks, my head, and my lips. They were washing the oxygen out of the air. I ducked my head and tried to move my arms to cover my face, but couldn't. The side of my head roared. Bile rose up in my throat.

Beside me, someone groaned. I struggled to open my eyes. Something pressed on my face, filled up my nostrils. I twisted my head and lifted against the pressure. My eyelids fluttered open to blackness, but the rain of dirt continued.

"Doug, you can't do this!" a muffled voice pleaded. "You aren't thinking straight."

"It has to happen. For you and me. Celeste, I love you."

I tried to shift my body, but earth pressed in. My nose filled with it. I pushed up against the weight. More and more dirt rained down, harder and heavier. I clenched my teeth. The pain in my head pounded. I tried to move my fingers and my arms. I felt warm flesh. Sam.

We were buried, together.

Panic exploded. I twisted and shoved, trying to push the soil off of our bodies, but my attempt at movement only caused the loose earth to pack harder around me, pinning my arms and legs. I sucked in a breath and pea-sized bits of dirt filled my nose.

"They'll search! This isn't over, Doug. They'll find the bodies."

"And we'll be as surprised as they are." Doug laughed. "Believe me, I've fine-tuned the art of fooling people."

Something pounded the earth above me. I tucked my face

against my arm and breathed in the tiny sheltered space. The earth around me shook as Doug stomped on my grave.

"Does that include me?"

"No, babe. I love you. It's all about you and me, being together." In the silence that followed, I imagined the two of them kissing a few feet above us while Sam and I suffocated below the ground.

"We'll head back to her cabin and pack up their belongings." The voices suddenly began to fade.

Were they moving away?

"You've been seen with her haven't you? No one will think anything about you helping her out." Doug laughed. "If anyone asks, we'll tell them Jamie decided to go back to Pawhuska. She was meeting Sam there."

"But she would have paid for the cabin, wouldn't she?"

"While you go pack up their things, I'll go to the office and cover the desk. Then I'll check Ms. Aldrich out of the cabin and leave cash to cover her stay. What we're about to recover will more than make up for the $250 rent."

Using my back, I lifted up against the pressure of the earth. A tiny space opened, enough for a few more breaths. My ears rang; every inch of me trembled. I was not going to die here. This wasn't the way my life would end. I slowed my breathing. *Calm down, Jamie.*

"It's risky, Doug. And I feel horrible about this."

"You know how much we need that money. My wife took everything I had in the divorce." Doug's voice took on a new angry tone. "This is our new start."

"Think what you're doing, Doug. You still don't know exactly where the money is or if it's even here. Don't let them die," Celeste pleaded.

I strained to hear the conversation going on above ground. The voices grew fainter, and a new sound reached me. Doug Moyer was digging somewhere else. Searching for the gangsters' loot?

"Don't you get it? I have to. They'll tell the cops everything," Moyer growled. "The money is somewhere close. She told me so on the way here."

"I hate this, Doug. There has to be another way."

"There's not. If I'd had only a few minutes more last Thursday night, Bridget would have told me and none of this would have happened."

A different sound reached my ears, barely more than a vibration in the earth. Scratching, snuffling, and a tiny shift in the earth packed in around me. I heard a whine.

Queenie?

"I don't understand what happened with Bridget." Celeste's voice was faint. "If it was an accident, why did she die?"

"Babe, pull your head out. You still don't get it. She wouldn't tell me, so I hit her and she went down. I thought she'd fainted so I searched the shack. She snuck out of some tunnel and took off. Hours later, I was still searching when I ran into Jamie and Sam and we found her body."

Beneath the ground, I squinted into the dark, fighting against the roaring pain in my head and the nausea it brought. "Queenie, I'm here. Find me. Find Sam," I whispered. Queenie's digging picked up speed.

"I cared about Bridget, Doug," Celeste said, her voice shaking and sounding very far away. "When I saw her lying there beneath that branch, I couldn't help but scream. If I had known you were so close, I wouldn't have taken off."

"It's okay, babe. It was easier for me to cover it up without you there. This way, nobody has a clue you and me are in this together."

"Together? But I didn't hurt Bridget, and I didn't throw that old busybody over the wall. You did!"

"Betty was a snoop, obsessed with that story about that kid who jumped back in the fifties. No one else had ever made the connection between my uncle and me, but the very first time she saw me last week, she saw my resemblance to Uncle Patrick."

Uncle Patrick? I twisted in the soft earth and pushed

toward the sound of Queenie's scratching. Bits of soil dribbled down around my head. I sensed more than heard Queenie's continued digging as a vibration through the ground.

"My mother told me that if my eyes were a little wider and my eyebrows less bushy, I'd be the spittin' image of my uncle. But Bridget couldn't see it, and neither did Aiden Blunt. If Snyder got wind of who I was and why I was here, five years of searching would be over. I have to find it now, babe. It's close. I know it. Jamie wanted to come to this exact place! If I have to dig up this whole area, I will." The shovel clinked against something. "What's this?"

Queenie whined only a few inches from my head. Her feet worked at the ground around me. I worked with her, rising up as she loosened the earth. Finally, the earth fell off me and into the shallow grave where Doug had buried me; I sat up. I went to my knees and elbows, then pulled myself completely up out of the grave. I glanced to one side, shaking my head and blinking my eyes. Many yards away, Celeste and Doug were head to head, bent over close to the wall, examining something.

I swiped dirt from my eyes. Queenie continued to dig; she had exposed most of Sam's body now. She licked at his face.

I had to do something. Any second, Doug or Celeste would see me. Doug might attack with the shovel again. Nearby lay one of the bricks from the old wall. I curled my fingers around it.

In one swift motion, I rose to my feet and ran toward the pair, throwing the brick as hard as I could at Doug's head.

Celeste lifted up, saw the brick coming and gasped.

Doug glanced my way and the heavy brick struck his face dead on. He collapsed, knocking Celeste down; his arms and legs splayed in all directions.

I grabbed another brick and crouched, waiting for him to get up. Celeste wiggled beneath his weight, finally shoving off his body and rolling away. She climbed to her feet.

"Jamie? I thought you were dead!" she stumbled toward

me. "I didn't know Doug had attacked Bridget. I didn't know he was after her money." She wrapped her arms around herself; her body trembled. "Oh, my God. I'm so stupid."

"Call for help. And don't let him get up." I grabbed the shovel and rushed back to Sam to help Queenie dig the remaining dirt off Sam's body once again.

Celeste spoke rapidly into her radio. "I need help, southeast forest, off trail." She gave the GPS coordinates of our location.

Queenie yipped, and Sam groaned.

"Oh, my God." I grabbed Sam's arms and pulled him up. I glanced at Moyer. He lay motionless, his face smashed and bleeding. Celeste watched him, her eyes red. She held a brick in her hand.

Sam sputtered, spit dirt, and struggled to sit upright. Dirt clods dropped from his hair and clothing.

"Sam, look at me." I brushed at his hair and then his clothing.

His eyes opened, and he blinked. I wiped the dirt from around his eyes.

"You're okay. Oh, my God, Sam. You're okay." I clutched him to me. Queenie tried to nose her way in between us, her tongue licking anything it could reach.

I glanced over my shoulder at Celeste, who now sat on the ground next to Doug.

"Doug?" she asked softly as she reached down to feel for a pulse on his neck. "They're coming. They're on the way."

She leaned over Doug, brushing the hair away from the oozing wound on his face. Her body shook with silent sobs.

CHAPTER 34

I took a sip of the tepid coffee Snyder poured for Celeste and me at the park office. Across the table from me, Celeste hunkered over her coffee cup, her eyes red and her face ashen. John Standingbear stood at the corner of the table.

"So, what you're telling me is that Doug Moyer went through ranger training and signed on for the sole purpose of finding this gangster loot his grandfather supposedly dug up and then reburied?" Standingbear asked.

Celeste nodded. "I swear I didn't know what he was up to. He'd been so preoccupied after Bridget was found, and even more so when Sam Mazie went missing."

"And he killed Bridget and Betty Wood because of this money?" Standingbear pressed.

"He almost succeeded in killing Sam, Stephen, and me, too," I added.

"His grandfather buried the money back in the thirties," Celeste continued. "He thought Bridget knew where it was. Last Thursday night, he went to her hut. They argued, and he hit her."

"And you're telling me you had nothing to do with any of this? You were there just before she was found." Snyder scowled.

"The limb crashed while I was taking my morning hike. When I saw Bridget, I screamed, and ran to get help." Celeste cupped her mug in her hands.

"Didn't you hear us calling?" I fidgeted in my chair. I needed to be at the hospital with Sam. I would have already been there if the sheriff had not insisted that I be present when he and Snyder interviewed Celeste.

"I heard Doug on the radio, calling for help as I rushed to the office. Poor Bridget." Celeste clasped her hands together. "Doug thought Stephen Knapp might know where the money was. He and Sam were cousins, so ..." She glanced at me. "I think Doug set the smoke bombs to lure you and Sam out of the cabin." She fingered her coffee cup. "Stephen showed up and Doug tricked them into leaving the cabin area with him. He thought they would lead him to the money."

I chewed on my lip. "And he imprisoned them even though they knew nothing?"

Celeste nodded. Her voice trembled. "Somehow, Stephen got away."

"And came to my cabin." I wondered how Stephen was now, and I thought of Sam. When they loaded him into the ambulance, he'd been so pale. His eyes were bloodshot and every inch of him was filthy.

Snyder leaned over the table and scrutinized me. "How are you feeling, Jamie?"

"I'll be all right. Soon. I need to get into town to Sam." I gingerly touched first my cheek, where the bee sting still throbbed, and my head, where the EMT had cleaned and bandaged my wound before leaving the park with Sam. The second ambulance, which took Doug Moyer to the hospital, had had a police escort.

"And I'll be right behind you," Sheriff Standingbear said. "I need to know exactly how Stephen fits into all this. He was seen acting suspiciously in the vicinity of Bridget's cabin after her death, and it was known that the two of them argued on more than one occasion. I need an explanation from both Stephen and Sam." Standingbear turned to Celeste. "And as for you, don't leave the area. The D.A. will want to interview you. He'll have to decide whether to charge you as an accessory after the fact."

Celeste nodded grimly.

"Then I'll see you there, Sheriff." I smiled at Celeste as I rose from the table. "I don't blame you for any of this. Now don't blame yourself."

Thirty minutes later, the sheriff and I walked into the Bartlesville hospital.

"I think we're all very lucky this had a happy ending for you and Sam," Sheriff John Standingbear said as we stepped off the elevator. "It could have been bad."

I knew it could have been worse than bad: Stephen, Sam and I could all be dead.

"Can you tell me what happened? How did you wind up buried at the old hideout?" Standingbear asked. He stood to one side of Sam's bed.

I sat on the edge of the mattress, as close as I could get to Sam. He was still pale, but he'd been bathed and bandaged, and the IV was already pumping him full of fluids.

"My cousin Stephen told me about some gangsters' loot he said was buried at the apiary. He thought Bridget had been killed because of it, and he didn't know who to trust." He closed his eyes and rubbed his face with one hand. "That night, when the cabin was filled with smoke, Doug Moyer called out to me from the cabin's back door. Once I was outside, he convinced me to go with him, saying Stephen had been injured at the apiary. I started around the cabin to tell you but Doug must have grabbed me. When I came to, I was bound and gagged. So was Stephen." His voice faltered.

"Take another drink, honey." I scooted the water glass toward him.

He swallowed a few sips before continuing. "Moyer would

come in and kick Stephen around, trying to get him to tell him where the money was. Stephen kept telling him he didn't know. Moyer beat Stephen and left him for dead. But Stephen crawled out." Sam felt the bandage on his head. "That's all I remember until Jamie dug me out of the ground."

Standingbear rubbed one ear lobe. "All of this because of some gangster treasure that's probably long gone?"

A few hours later, Sam talked the doctor into releasing him.

"I don't need to be in the hospital, Jamie. I need something to eat, a soft bed, and you. Not necessarily in that order."

"You've got it. And not necessarily in that order."

Back at the cabin, I helped Sam climb into bed. I slipped off my jeans and T-shirt, donned my nightshirt, and climbed in next to him. "I know you need something to eat, but I need to feel close to you more." I snuggled in.

Sam's breathing slowed. "Do you think there is loot out there, left by the gangsters?"

I nodded. "Mother told me she and Bridget helped bury it. But I think Bridget's been spending the money all these years. If there's anything left, it's probably in her cabin."

"But it's been searched. By more than one person," he said softly.

"Yes. But I have a feeling I might know where it is. And it will stay safe until we get there."

Sam's breathing deepened and slowed. I studied his bruised face, touching each bandage with the tip of my finger. *Thank you, God.* He began to snore softly. I slipped out of bed, dug my cell phone out of my purse, and called Cindy.

"Stephen's still in ICU," she explained. "There was internal bleeding, so they operated. The doctor says he will make a full recovery. They'll move him to a regular room day after tomorrow, I hope."

"Are you staying at the hospital overnight?"

"No. Now that Stephen is stable, I need to be at home with the kids."

"Okay. Call me when you head home. I need to borrow a few things."

CHAPTER 35

Wednesday, May 22

"Sam? Feel like getting out of bed?" I asked when Sam opened his eyes the next morning. I'd been hovering over him, hoping to see him stir. Finally, at 8 a.m., I sat on the edge of the bed and watched his face. The technique had worked for my kids, Alison and Matt, when they were little and wanted me to wake up—why not for me now?

"Hm?" He blinked and closed his eyes again.

"Feel like finding a treasure?" I whispered.

His eyes popped open again. "What?"

"A treasure? The loot? First, we have to go pick up Stephen's beekeeping equipment."

"Don't tell me it involves bees. Surely you don't want another close encounter of the bee kind." He reached out and touched the itching red bump on my cheek.

I resisted the urge to scratch that sting, as well as the one on the back of my hand and the back of my neck. "This will be a good experience. I promise. Get dressed. Think you can manage a short hike in the woods?"

Fifteen minutes later, Sam and I climbed into the truck. I drove out of the park, to Stephen's house. Cindy was waiting for us on the front porch.

"Here's the stuff you wanted to borrow. What are you going to do?" Cindy squinted at us from the shady porch.

"We're checking Bridget's hut for the money, Cindy. Last time I was there, the place was full of bees."

Her eyes widened. "Bees? Inside her hut? Be careful."

The roads of the park, both public and service, were familiar to me now. I took the one that would bring us the closest to Bridget's hut. We parked, and then trekked through the forest to the shack. This time, I knew exactly how to get where I was going.

Birds chirped in the trees above us, and a squirrel chattered from the end of a long limb before leaping across to another tree. Above the tree canopy, bits of puffy clouds scuttled across the bright blue sky.

"Be on the lookout for traps. Apparently, Bridget set some to keep trespassers away."

We picked our way through the sumac grove and tall dewy grasses to the hidden hut.

"Here. Put your gear on." I pulled gloves and netted hat from my backpack. "Those bees have been trapped in the hut a full day now. They won't be happy."

Sam grinned at me as he put on the hat. "This is not what I expected to be doing today. But if you think you know where Bridget stashed that loot, let's find it." He studied the hut's hidden façade.

A large branch had been wedged against the door, preventing anyone from opening it from either side. I zipped up my windbreaker, pulled the branch aside, and opened the door slowly. "Stand back."

A few bees buzzed slowly out into the sunlight, followed by more, and more. When the slow parade stopped, I peered inside the dimly lit hut. A few bee bodies littered the top of the bed as well as the floor. I broke off a leafy branch and cleared a path on the floor before we stepped inside.

Sam ducked to pass through the doorway, then gazed around at the well-organized interior. "A place for everything and everything in its place. So where do you think the loot is?

You've already checked the trunk, and I bet you weren't the only one who did."

I shoved the material away from the windows and pulled the cord to uncover the skylight. Light flooded the little hut.

"I'm thinking it's here." I reached toward the pyramid of thick candles on the lowest shelf, pulled out several from the front row, and checked the bottom surfaces. "Not this one. Or this one." I grabbed one farther back in the stack and smiled at the shape of a coin in the center of the candle. "Here." I handed the candle to Sam. "My guess is that each candle has ten or more coins inside. Moyer said they could be worth $40 each in today's market."

Sam whistled. "Bridget put all the money into the candles. When she needed it, she burned the candle for light and then took the coins to the bank." He began to count the pyramid of candles stacked neatly on the shelves. "Twelve candles wide, three candles deep, six candles high—that's over 200 candles. We can't leave them here."

"Let's fill up our packs and take them back to the cabin. We'll turn them over to the sheriff."

We dismantled the candle stack, and as we reached the bottom, we found that some of the candles had been tied together using long strips of dried grass. A note had been tucked down in between two of the top candles. I pulled it out and read:

"To my dearest friend, Mary Jamison. Patrick would have wanted you to have your share. Whatever he may have told you, you were his secret love, not Aiden."

EPILOGUE

Friday, May 24

After sleeping most of the day Thursday, both Sam and I were ready to join the world again. Sam's brown skin had regained a healthy color, and although his eye was still swollen, the swelling had gone down. Yellow tinged the purple bruise.

Sam and I drove to the group camp just before 11 a.m.

I didn't know who had arranged the memorial service for Bridget. We stood at the back of the room as dozens of people filed in to pay their respects, each with kind words to say about their former teacher and friend. Sheriff John Standing-bear attended, as did Celeste and Roy Snyder. Aiden Blunt shuffled up to the front of the room to give the eulogy.

When the brief ceremony was finished, Sheriff John Standingbear approached Sam and me. "In case you were wondering, Bernie Wood will be released from the hospital today," he said. "He'll return to Wichita with Betty's body. Doug Moyer is in jail. With two charges of murder, two charges of kidnapping and three charges of assault, he'll be in prison for the rest of his life." The sheriff cleared his throat. "And there's one more thing. I've been asked to let you know that Bridget left a will. It was kept in a safety deposit box at the bank. They would like to read the will this afternoon. Can you make it to Bartlesville by 2 p.m.?"

We entered the bank's conference room five minutes before 2 p.m. Sam was weary; he needed to be back in bed, resting, and

I didn't have much energy either. I wasn't sure why I'd been asked to be here. I'd never met Bridget, and although I did feel I knew her, after all I'd learned about her from Celeste and my mother, I could't imagine why Bridget's attorney would want me there.

"Thank you for coming," Timothy Werling, the bank president, said. He nodded at Sam and me. A few minutes later, Cindy and a heavily bandaged Stephen joined us. Stephen walked using a cane, Cindy held his other arm.

"I think some of you know Rodger Finnegan," Werling said. "He was Bridget Halsted's attorney. Upon notification of her death, he began to put her affairs in order. Bridget is one of those rare people who have no heirs. However, she did list two beneficiaries. The two of us were happy to learn that Ms. Halsted's missing beneficiary is represented today by Mary Jamison's daughter, Jamie Aldrich. I understand you are soon to be Mrs. Sam Mazie. Let me offer my congratulations." The bank president nodded at me.

"You can't know how relieved I was to learn who you were," Finnegan said. "Bridget spoke of your mother often. She was anxious that in the event of her death, your mother be found. The last we spoke of it, she had no idea where to begin to search for her."

My heart ached for Bridget and for my mother. I had narrowly missed an opportunity to meet and get to know this woman who had been my mother's good friend. She could have told me so much about my own mother's youth and the dreams she'd held dear to her heart so many years ago.

"I'll get right to the reason we are here. You all know that Bridget elected to live the last thirty-plus years as a recluse. Formerly employed as a teacher, she had saved little money to sustain her life away from the city. On the other hand, she required little. A modest inheritance left to her by her parents provided for most of her needs for many years." The attorney cleared his throat.

"Five years ago, she came to me and to Mr. Werling with a purse full of vintage silver dollars. She assured us she had done nothing illegal to obtain them; she had merely found them. In accordance with Oklahoma law, we determined that Ms. Halsted had every right to the coins she had found provided she paid a minimum income tax on the amount she cashed in each year."

Stephen sat forward in his chair. Cindy's eyes widened.

"Over the course of the past five years, Ms. Halsted cashed in many coins," Worthy continued. "Sam and Jamie found the remainder of them in Bridget's cabin." He paused and looked at Stephen and Cindy. "We have had the coins cleaned and evaluated. We know the worth of the coins in today's silver melt value: $60,000."

I drew in a breath. It was more than either Sam or I had expected.

"In addition," the attorney went on. "Ms. Halsted kept a safety deposit box here at the bank. Inside that box, she kept the stocks and bonds she had been purchasing with some of the proceeds from the sale of the coins."

Stocks and bonds? Mother had said Bridget was smart. Apparently, she was a savvy investor as well.

"That brings me back to Ms. Halsted's will. She listed only two beneficiaries. One-half of all her worldly goods goes to Stephen and Cindy Knapp, with a notation made that 'all debts are forgiven.' The other half goes to Mary Jamison, represented here by Jamie Aldrich. I have copies of the will for both of you as well as a death certificate. As for what this means for you, Stephen and Cindy, and to your mother, Jamie, we can go over in detail individually after this meeting concludes."

Cindy covered her face with her hands as Stephen slid his arms around her and hugged her close. "Oh, my God," she said.

"My mother will not believe this," I said to Sam. "How extraordinary."

He rubbed my upper arm absently with his hand. "It is. What if we hadn't gone to Osage Hills State Park? What if we had never found that inscription? And farther back than that, what if we had never met again last year? What if?"

"Too many what ifs,'" I interrupted. "It happened. It had to happen."

"Yes," Sam said. He kissed my cheek. "And there are other things that have to happen. Like our wedding. We have some planning to do."

"I'm not sure we need to plan. Why don't we just get married? Soon. At your church in Pawhuska. That beautiful Osage Cathedral." I rubbed one finger along his jawline.

Sam grinned.

As we left the bank, I plucked a yellow coreopsis growing in the flowerbed at the bank entrance, shooed away a hovering honeybee, and tucked the flower behind my ear.

About the Setting – Osage Hills State Park

Osage Hills State Park was one of Oklahoma's original seven state parks. Soon after the State Park Department was created in 1935, the site was selected to become a State park. CCC Company 895 moved here, and built the park between 1936 and 1940, one of 35 camps in the Oklahoma District of the Eighth Army Corps Area.

The park's 1100 acres is beautiful forested land located in the rolling hills of Osage County. The park includes 8 cabins (7 built by the CCC), picnic shelters, a swimming pool, a group camp with ten bunkhouses and a dining/meeting hall, a campground with 20 RV sites with electricity, and 25 primitive sites for camping. The park includes Lake Look-Out, which offers boat rentals and fishing, and a Look-Out Tower near the primitive camping sites.

Sand Creek winds through the property. Over time, the creek has created natural bluffs rising a hundred feet above the creek itself, and also natural waterfalls. Several miles of hiking trails exist, offering hikers a sampling of the diverse ecosystems found in the Osage Hills. These include tallgrass prairie remnants, post-oak/blackjack (crosstimbers) forest, and riverbottom forest.

Contact information: (918) 336-4141; email: OsageHills@ travelok.com; website: www.stateparks.com/osage_hills_ state_park_in_oklahoma.html

Address: 2131 Osage Hills Park Road, Pawhuska, OK 74056

About the Civilian Conservation Corps

The Civilian Conservation Corps was created in 1933, when the U.S. Congress enacted legislation to create this New Deal Program. It was developed in conjunction with the National Park Service to develop national and state parks which were accessible to all citizens. The CCC projects have become synonymous with distinctive architecture and quality craftsmanship. Many of the structures, which utilized materials (trees and stone) found locally, have survived the test of time.

The number of men allowed to participate in the program was determined by the population of each state. Nationwide, over 2 million men and boys participated. This Works Progress Administration program was intended to put the unemployed to work, and that work included projects designed to 'slow erosion, replant forests, build dams, bridges, buildings and parks, roads and trails, as well as install telephone line,' during The Great Depression.

This program did three things: it allowed people to regain their self-respect, feed their families and pursue employment. Each man received $30 a month for his efforts. The young men, who were selected for the program because they were unable to find work and had families they needed to support, were required to send $25 of that monthly salary home to their parents.

In Oklahoma, one-third of the families were on relief at that time. Statewide, over 5000 men worked in twenty-six CCC camps.

In 1935, Oklahoma appropriated 25,000 to create the State Park Commission, which would become the Division of State Parks. The first CCC camps in the state were created to create Oklahoma's first seven state parks.

The camp at Osage Hills State Park was occupied by Company 895, and included 189 young men between the ages of 18 and 23. When the men first arrived in 1935, they had to finish constructing their own camp facilities, which had been started by a team of local carpenters and laborers. Then they began constructing the park, building the roads and trails, clearing picnic areas and lawns. They assembled cabins, as well as picnic shelters, bathhouses and a community center at the group camp. The CCC Camp operated at Osage Hills from 1935 to July of 1941.

Seven different sites in Oklahoma were selected to become state parks built by the CCC. These sites were selected because they were accessible to most of the residents of the state, and were also in areas of historical or geological significance. The sites were diverse environmentally as well. Parks representing the humid, wooded areas of the state included Osage Hills in the northcentral part of the state, Robbers Cave near Wilburton in the east central portion, Spavinaw Hills in the northeast and Beaver's Bend near Idabel in the far southeast corner of the state. Roman Nose near Watonga in central Oklahoma, Boiling Springs near Woodward in the northwest, and Quartz Mountain near Lone Wolf in the southwest were representative of the more arid regions of Oklahoma.

In addition to the construction of new state park facilities, the WPA directed the CCC construction of many different types of buildings, including municipal parks, baseball stadiums, schools, gymnasiums, post offices, armories, court houses and city halls. In Oklahoma alone, 825 schools were built as well as several dams.

Many of these stone structures, still stand throughout the state of Oklahoma.

The Conservation Corps program allowed young men of the Depression era to feed their families not through a handout, but through a program that left an amazing legacy.

To learn more about the Citizen's Conservation Corps projects in Oklahoma, visit: http://www.ccclegacy.org/CCC_Camps_Oklahoma.html. For national information, visit: http://livingnewdeal.berkeley.edu.

Check your home state for information about the projects completed in your area.

About: Depression Era Gangster Pretty Boy Floyd

Many books and movies have been created about the infamous gangsters of the Depression Era. After the stock market crash of 1929, the Great Depression began. Franklin Delano Roosevelt was the President of the United States during those hard years. People who had invested in the stock market during its expansive growth during the 1920s (Post-World War I) lost everything. Many companies closed. Many people had no way to support themselves; they had no food to eat. In addition, Prohibition prevented the production, distribution and sale of alcoholic beverages, the country's favorite vice.

A new type of criminal activity began. These criminals, who may have begun their criminal careers as 'moonshiners'—making and selling illegal booze—began to rob small-town country banks and armored vehicles. These so-called Gangsters were everywhere throughout the Midwest.

Most frightening of all, they carried guns – automatic machine guns known as 'Tommy guns.' People were rarely injured in these robberies, but the newly formed Federal Bureau of Investigation was desperate to capture the robbers. John Dillinger became Public Enemy No. 1.

Gangsters frequented certain regions of the country, and Oklahoma and surrounding states had their share. One gang which operated in this region, as well as up into Kansas and to the Arkansas border, was the Cookson Hills Gang. Its most famous member, Charles Arthur Floyd, was also known as 'Pretty Boy.'

Floyd was also known as the "Robin Hood of the Cookson Hills" because he was known to give money and food to those in need. He had a cult following, particularly around the area of Sallisaw, OK, where he once lived.

Floyd killed a man and was badly wounded himself in a gun battle in Bixby, OK in 1932, but his life of crime continued until he was killed in a shoot-out with the FBI in Ohio in 1934.

By 1935, all of the most-wanted gangsters, including "Baby Face" Nelson, Bonnie and Clyde and "Machine Gun" Kelly, had been caught or killed.

From the Author

Writing has provided an outlet for my busy imagination ever since I learned to write in the second grade. Although I have always worked professionally in jobs requiring extensive writing ability, it is writing fiction that makes my muse dance.

While working as a historic park planner and naturalist for the Oklahoma Tourism and Recreation Department, the pairing of history and mystery solidified in my writing. Then, as a special feature writer for the Ponca City News in the late 1980s, my love of little known places and ordinary people expanded.

Everyone has a story, every place has a life of its own. The writer's job is to ferret out that story and that life and make it real for the reader.

—*Mary Coley*

CPSIA information can be obtained at www.ICGtesting.com
Printed in the USA
BVOW08s0727151115

427091BV00001B/33/P

9 781627 873130